SURVIVAL

Look for other REMNANTS™
titles by K.A. Applegate:

Also by K.A. Applegate:

ANIMORPHS ®

REMNANTS™

SURVIVAL

K.A. APPLEGATE

AN
APPLE
PAPERBACK

SCHOLASTIC INC.
New York Toronto London Auckland Sydney
Mexico City New Delhi Hong Kong Buenos Aires

ISBN 0-590-87735-6

12 11 10 9 8 7 6 5 4 3 2   4 5 6 7 8/0

Printed in the U.S.A.   40
First printing, July 2003

For Michael and Jake

SURVIVAL

CHAPTER ONE

"YOU COULD HAVE PREVENTED THIS."

Tate turned to face the door.

There, in the gloom of the immense doorway, a darker shadow. Still, silent, watching her.

It was Yago. And in that split second, Tate knew.

The little seedling that had filled Jobs with hope for new life on Earth was a fake. A trick. Yago and the Troika had created it and used it to lure everyone onto the surface. The seedling was nothing more than part of an elaborate plan to hijack the ship.

Fear rushed through her. Jobs, Mo'Steel, Billy, 2Face, the others — they were all stuck on the ashy, dead planet. They had little water, practically no food. And they were going to die unless she did something to help them.

She was their only chance. She was alone on the

ship with the bad guys: Amelia, Duncan, Charlie — and Yago.

When had they joined forces? Didn't matter.

Why would Amelia cut a deal with Yago? That didn't matter, either.

Four against one. Not such hot odds. That mattered.

"You can leave now," Yago ordered. A giggle escaped and he put a hand to his mouth. Weird. He was acting manic, cartoonish, crazy.

Tate hesitated. Her thoughts were jumbled. The viewscreens showed Earth below them, still close. She could see Violet and D-Caf and the others, all looking up at the ship. They were close enough that she could make out their stunned expressions. They were helpless. No way for them to do anything from the planet's surface.

Could she tackle Yago? Yes, she could do that or — or worse. But he didn't seem to be controlling the ship. Amelia must be doing that from somewhere down in the basement.

Okay. Tate had to get down there. She had to stop Amelia somehow. Forget about Yago. He was just a distraction.

Yago stood aside and Tate walked slowly from

the bridge, wondering if her fury would make the Mouth appear and half-hoping that it would.

The Mouth was a mutation. Somehow — Tate didn't understand how — she'd changed, or been altered, in the five hundred years since she'd left Earth. Maybe low-level radiation had twisted her DNA as she lay sleeping in her crude hibernation berth aboard the shuttle. Maybe the mutation would have occurred even if they hadn't been sucked into this much bigger ship.

Maybe. But Tate suspected Mother had something to do with the mutation. When you came right down to it, Mother was mixed up in most things that had happened since they woke up from their five-hundred-year sleep.

Mother was the massive alien ship that surrounded Tate. A ship the size of Detroit. She'd been a home to the handful of people who'd escaped Earth just before an asteroid rammed into the planet and destoyed seven billion people. A home — or a prison. Depended on how you looked at it.

Mother was also the computer that ran the ship — the ship's consciousness, personality, brain. A computer so advanced she could feel loneliness, could plan strategy, could exercise free will.

Mother was a power. That's why the scared, lost band of Remnants had been fighting for control of her ever since they'd mysteriously woken up here. They'd fought aliens in the beginning — and when they'd finally managed to overpower most of the aliens, they began fighting one another.

Tate hadn't seen this last move coming, though. She hadn't expected the hijacking. She'd never dreamed Amelia, Duncan, and Charlie would form an alliance with Yago. Yago had fooled them all into thinking he was insane. Or, maybe he'd fooled the Troika into thinking he was sane.

"You haven't won yet, Yago," Tate told herself. "This game isn't over until I'm dead." She came out into the still, echoing corridor. The elevator was directly ahead of her — maybe two hundred yards away. Tate sprinted for it, expecting to be stopped, attacked.

Her back quivered with nerves and she had to fight an urge to keep looking over her shoulder. Yago had a gun.

Tate was still about fifty yards from the elevator when the ship accelerated upward awkwardly, knocking her to her knees. Amelia — somehow Tate was sure it was Amelia and not Charlie or Duncan — was flying the ship with the skill of a clumsy child. Tate hoped she didn't crash the thing.

A low moan, a sound of suffering, rose up around Tate until she was engulfed in sound. It came from the walls, the floor, the air. The sound was soft at first, but grew quickly in intensity until Tate clasped her hands to her ears to block it out.

Mother was crying.

The ground under Tate's feet shook. A hot, dry wind sprang up from nowhere. The towering walls of the fortress Billy had built to protect them vibrated and began to break up into chunks.

"Bad," Tate mumbled as the wind forced her to her knees, then down onto the floor. "This is very bad."

The environment Billy had created was dying. That had to mean — what? That Amelia had somehow severed Billy's connection to Mother? That Billy was dead? He was down there on the surface with the others. Had someone just attacked him?

Worry and guilt stabbed Tate. "You could have prevented this," she told herself angrily. She could have saved Billy and ruined Yago's plan.

They'd been on the bridge. Tate, 2Face, Billy, and Mo'Steel. Tate felt as if a long time had passed since then, but probably it had been less than ten minutes ago.

Billy and 2Face had argued. 2Face wanted Billy to go down to the surface to see the little seedling that had filled Jobs with hope for new life on Earth. Billy had resisted and 2Face had bullied him off the ship. Tate knew 2Face enjoyed showing her power, flaunting her influence over Billy.

So why didn't I stand up for him? Tate wondered. Billy had earned her loyalty. The deadly, bloody war with the aliens — the Meanies and Riders and Squids — had ended only because Mother had chosen to merge with Billy's mind.

Who knows why? Maybe Mother "loved" Billy — if you believed a computer could feel love. Maybe Billy was her only choice, the one living thing on the ship smart enough to communicate with her without going mad. Whatever the reason, Billy's relationship with Mother had allowed him to protect the Remnants, to create food for them, to build walls for them.

Billy had kept them all alive.

So why had Tate let 2Face bully him?

"Stupid," Tate muttered at the floor. "Lazy. Stupid."

As if agreeing with her, the wind picked up. Tate

was caught in the middle of a tornado. Debris swirled around her head. Fast. Then slow. Then fast. A chunk of something glanced off her shoulder, whacked her ear, and went skidding across the floor.

The walls Billy had created kept dissolving, revealing the monumental geometric architecture of the alien-designed ship. Tate cowered on the floor, hands over her head, until the wind abated and the savage moaning let up somewhat.

As soon as she was able, Tate stumbled to her feet and ran for the elevator. How much time had she lost? Three minutes? Five? She didn't know. Too long. Anything could be happening on Earth. She had to get control of the ship and get back to her friends.

Mother was picking up speed now, moving more smoothly. They'd probably already traveled thousands of miles.

Tate reached the elevator. She half-expected it to be disabled. Yago could have pulled the plug, flipped the switch. Or Amelia. But when Tate stepped onto the platform, it immediately dropped away, silently and fast enough to make her nauseous.

This was normal. This was good. A ride on the elevator always made Tate feel like vomiting. Mother hadn't been built for humans. Aliens that resembled overgrown translucent starfish had built her. Ship-wrights. Apparently the Shipwrights didn't have very sensitive inner ears. They liked a good fast drop.

The elevator stopped. Tate moved cautiously into the basement. The "basement" — that was their nick-name for the lowest level of the ship.

Tate wasn't particularly fond of the basement. She tried to avoid going down there. She was from L.A. City femme. She knew how to navigate a grid of streets. She could handle gangs of punks, or turf wars at the local mall. These things she under-stood.

Wide-open spaces weren't her thing. And the basement was essentially ten to twenty square miles of nothing. In all that space, there were only a cou-ple of scattered enclosures, a few pits with comput-ers. The exterior walls of the ship were so far off, Tate couldn't even see them.

Tate turned quickly to the right, then the left — scanning the vast expanse surrounding her. No sign of Amelia or the others. Maybe they were in their mysterious hideout, the corner of the basement where they'd hidden from the rest of the Remnants for some private reason. Made sense.

Walking there would take half a day. By the time

she got there, Jobs and the others would probably be — but Tate couldn't think about that.

The others were tough, she reminded herself. They'd survived battles and sieges. They could handle being marooned on Earth for a few hours. She just had to find Amelia quickly. She headed off in what she hoped was the right direction.

"To us," Amelia said. She smiled slyly at Yago.

"To us," Duncan and Charlie echoed mechanically. They were smiling steadily at Yago, too. Their expressions were dreamy, almost — hungry.

Yago lifted an imaginary glass. "Cheers!" he said with a sarcastic smirk. "Too bad we don't have any champagne for the toast. Then again, maybe that's for the best since we don't have any glasses, either."

Yago was being a brat. Ruining the celebration. He knew that, but he couldn't help himself. He was grumpy. He had a dull headache behind his eyes. Low blood sugar, felt like. He needed a snack.

But even something as simple as having a snack was impossible because the food had disappeared along with everything else Billy had created. Yago had foreseen this problem way back when they'd first discussed tossing Billy off the ship. He'd raised his concerns. Amelia had promised to handle it. But now they were sitting at one of the Shipwrights' ugly too-tall tables with nothing in front of them except dust. Maybe not even dust.

Forget champagne. Yago wanted a soda. His throat was dry and slightly sore. He wanted ice cream. Preferably soft-serve.

"Vanilla chocolate swirl with jimmies," Yago said challengingly. "Is that too much to ask? 'Cause if it is, I could make do with an ice-cream sandwich."

Amelia smiled coyly, as if Yago had made a charming joke. The other two stared benignly back at him, expressions fixed. Their faces were blank screens. Nobody home.

Yago turned his gaze on Charlie. "You hungry at all?"

No reply. Charlie seemed to be daydreaming. His brain was somewhere far, far away.

Yago ran a hand in front of Duncan's face. He didn't even blink.

Yago raised an eyebrow. "They okay?" he asked Amelia suspiciously.

"Just tired," Amelia soothed him. "The last few days have been — stressful. For all of us."

"Yeah," Yago said, sitting back uneasily. Amelia hadn't mentioned Tate yet. That little screw-up, that little problem. Their stowaway. Well, he certainly wasn't about to bring it up. Let Amelia take responsibility.

"I was worried that seedling wouldn't fool them," Yago said. "Especially Billy Weird. Guess he wasn't as smart as I thought."

"He's very smart," Amelia said matter-of-factly. "It's just that you're smarter."

Yago rocked back and forth, trying to lull himself, wanting to let Amelia's praise just wash over him. Nothing doing.

Amelia — there was something wrong with Amelia. Yago couldn't quite grasp it, but something —

She was a good-looking femme. Long dark hair. Sparkling gray eyes. Slim figure. Amelia was definitely the best-looking femme onboard.

Only — well, suddenly it seemed to Yago that there was something wrong with her mouth.

Her tongue.

That was it.

Somehow her tongue seemed too large, too mobile. Yago stopped rocking. He wondered if he'd been hasty casting off Violet, Olga, Noyze, and 2Face. It seemed the best-looking femme onboard was hiding some weird secrets.

CHAPTER TWO

MOTHER WAS NO PLACE TO SHOW WEAKNESS.

Amazing, Charlie thought.

He could *see.* Not just perfectly — superhumanly. As if his cerebral cortex were plugged into a scanning electron microscope. Yago was now a trillion vibrating cells. Charlie could even see *inside* the cells where the mitochondria floated dreamily around their hairy nuclei.

This was *cool.* He'd always had poor eyesight. He'd been "four eyes" all through school and those endless summers at camp. Sometimes kids could really be jerks. Although, come to think of it, his roommates at the loony bin had called him "four eyes," too. Well, what did that prove? Charlie supposed it proved adults could be jerks, too. Not exactly a stunning revelation.

Thank god he'd sucked it up and gotten that laser surgery a couple of months before the Rock hit. Wouldn't want to be "four eyes" on Mother. Mother was no place to show weakness — not even a reliance on contact lens solution.

Well. No need to worry about *that* anymore. He wasn't "four eyes" any longer. In fact, he wasn't even sure how long he'd be "two eyes."

"I — am — evolving!" Charlie sang to himself in a theatrical mezzo-soprano.

"*Why are you so happy?*" Duncan asked in grumpy mindvoice. "*Suddenly we've got insect-o-vision and it won't turn off. Ask me, that's not very evolved.*"

Charlie ignored Duncan. A matter of principle.

He didn't like having Duncan whining in his head. He didn't like having Duncan in his head, period. Let Amelia and Duncan play with their mindvoices. Charlie wasn't interested. If he had something to say, he'd open his mouth and say it. At least, as long as he had a mouth.

Besides, he was busy studying Yago's cells. Amelia was handling Yago. Slowly revealing his new station in life, letting him down easy. That left Charlie free to stare. Charlie wasn't sure which was more enticing — studying a single cell in all of its gorgeous detail or pulling back for a wide shot of the entire glorious collection.

Those cells could stop his thirst and control the

pounding in his head. Turns out, turning into some nameless creature wasn't all fun and games. He was getting bigger and more complex by the minute — which Amelia assured him was a good thing. But his cells couldn't divide fast enough to keep up with demand. Eventually his body would reach equilibrium. But until then — things were mighty uncomfortable.

Charlie subtly shifted closer to Yago. Maybe if he was fast, he could get to him before Amelia noticed. Once the cells were absorbed, she wouldn't be able to do anything about it.

"*Not yet,*" came Amelia's voice in his head. She sounded amused, even loving. "*Soon, but not yet. We need him for now.*"

Charlie thought some very unkind things about Amelia — she shouldn't be able to hear what he was *thinking*! That wasn't *moral*, that wasn't *right*. Then he remembered that she could hear even *that*.

"Our time is coming," Amelia said. She sounded so smug, Yago wanted to laugh in her face.

The Troika — that's what the other Remnants called Amelia, Charlie, and Duncan — liked to brag about how they were evolving into "higher beings."

Whatever. Maybe they were. So far, Yago wasn't

impressed. Duncan and Charlie looked like zombies with their vacant stares. Even worse, they looked fat. Bloated. Not pretty. Like they were retaining water, maybe. And Amelia — well, Yago refused to think about what was happening with her tongue.

"Our evolution is picking up speed," Amelia stated serenely.

"Hey, great," Yago said with a roll of his eyes so subtle Amelia probably didn't even notice it. "I'm happy for you. Let me know if I can do anything to help."

"Actually, I was just getting to that," Amelia said smoothly.

Yago raised one eyebrow. Amelia knew him well enough to understand she'd have to pay for any favor he granted her. He pretended to be indifferent. But, actually, he was eagerly considering what he could get out of the deal. He wouldn't negotiate for food — Amelia had already promised him that and he intended to hold her to her promise.

But what about Tate? Someone had to go after her, track her down, and — deal with her. Yago preferred to stay as far away from the Mouth as possible. That was just common sense. He'd tell Amelia to send one of her flunkies. Let Duncan or Charlie risk their lives. Yago's was too precious.

"How can I help?" Yago asked graciously. He would be dignified about this. Let Amelia keep her pride.

"You will bring all of the living creatures on board to us," Amelia said calmly. "You see, as we evolve, we're getting bigger. More — dense. We require additional material in the form of living cells."

"What?" Yago snorted, unable to believe what he was hearing. Forget about the freaky-monster stuff. Amelia actually had the audacity to give him orders? "You want *me* to go round up the Meanies and Riders?" he demanded rudely. "If you need more cells, then why don't —"

Yago didn't finish the sentence because he suddenly found himself on the floor, unable to breathe. Amelia was right in his face, hovering over him, eyes wild. How had she gotten so close so fast? Yago hadn't even seen her move.

Yago gasped, or tried to. No air entered his lungs. None escaped. Something — something was squeezing. Crushing his Adam's apple. His hands went to his throat.

Something was wrapped around his neck. He clawed at it, desperate to pry it loose, wanting air. What the — it felt like a moist, bumpy snake — oh, god, it was Amelia's tongue! That's why she was hovering over him! Yago's head swam with dizziness and disgust.

His lungs burned. He tried to control himself, tried to think, tried to act like a man. . . .

He kicked, but his legs flailed uselessly, connecting with nothing. He shoved at Amelia's shoulders. She didn't budge.

He gasped. Nothing.

Gasped. Not working . . .

His vision was narrowing, blackness creeping up at the edges. He felt his legs start to relax.

Then the blackness receded. Amelia sat back, and Yago was assaulted by the sight of her tongue oozily slipping back into her mouth like an overgrown snail retreating into its shell.

"Will you help us?" Amelia asked sweetly.

Yago didn't reply. He stared up at her, breathing in deep, rasping breaths and massaging his bruised throat. Breathing was still difficult. It hurt — she'd done something to him, damaged him somehow. Turned him into another freak.

"Do it," Amelia said less kindly, "or you'll be the first to be absorbed."

Yago nodded numbly. Now he really wanted a soda.

*   *   *

Tate walked until her mind quieted and stopped cir-cling around and around her worries — were the Remnants who were abandoned on Earth dead? Was Yago about to attack her? How would she survive without food or water?

She kept walking until the sound of her foot-steps made her whimper with aggravation and the doubts crowded back in. She was alone! Her friends had to be dead by now! She would be dead, too, soon.

Her legs were tired. Her big toe pushed through the top of one of her ragged gym shoes. The nail on that toe ached. Her throat felt like sandpaper. Her eventual confrontation with Amelia or Yago or Charlie or Duncan played in her mind like a bad horror movie.

The Troika was dangerous.

Violent.

Ruthless.

Charlie had destroyed Kubrick by turning him-self into some sort of freaky porcupine with deadly needle quills. She didn't want to die the way Kubrick had died. . . .

And Amelia . . . Tate would never forget the sight of Amelia turning into a seething collection of pus and bacteria and filth caustic enough to melt a Blue Meanie into nothingness.

Tate had never seen Duncan. She didn't know if he was a killer. If he had mutations. But considering the company he was keeping, she definitely had her suspicions.

Tate told herself she should be scared, but she wasn't really frightened. What she felt was — numb.

She kept walking, all the time uncomfortably aware that if Amelia was hiding in one of the computer pits, she would be able to see her coming from a long way off.

Well, too bad. She couldn't sneak up on Amelia when she didn't even know where Amelia was. Or what she was.

Tate walked on. She couldn't think of anything else to do. She was completely unprepared for a fight — or even for a long walk. She had no water. No food. No weapons. No plan. She wasn't clear on what she was going to do if and when she managed to find Amelia or figure out who was controlling Mother. She had no idea how to pilot the ship. No clue of how to once again locate Earth in the inky expanse of space.

Under different circumstances, the walk might

have been boring. There wasn't much to see. Up above was the massive glass ceiling. When Tate had seen it last, the enormous space had been filled with an environment Mother had created for the savage two-headed Riders. Copper-colored water. An occasional island. Trees with too-pliant trunks and branches. An otherworldly landscape, but beautiful in its way.

Now the world above was as dry, barren, and sad as a fishbowl after all of the fishies are gone. Tate wondered if any of the Riders were still alive. Somehow that seemed hard to imagine. The ship was so silent, so still that it was easier to believe she was entirely alone.

The ship felt like a tomb. The only sounds she could hear were a low hum of the hull vibrating as the ship slipped through space — that, and her own footsteps.

Tate plodded on, suddenly wondering if Amelia and Yago weren't coming after her because they were dead, too. Now Tate felt her first quivers of fear. Maybe she was the last human alive in the universe.

Hours later, Tate finally reached the corner of the ship. She squatted on the hard metallic floor and pressed her aching back against the riveted seam where the ceiling came down and met the floor.

She stared out over the vast, utterly still basement. And she began to cry.

She was hungry. Thirsty. Tired beyond belief. Her chest throbbed with loneliness. She felt guilty and disappointed that she hadn't come up with a better plan to help her friends.

It was too late to help them now.

She had to admit that.

She had to face the fact that she had failed them. She had to face the fact that there was literally nobody left in the universe who wished her well or wanted her to survive.

She wished — she wished she had stayed on Earth with her dog, Lily, in her apartment, five hundred years ago. Stayed at home when the Rock hit.

Tate let herself drift.

Sometimes she dozed off. That was nice. She looked forward to sleeping, to the release. When she was awake, she sat against the same wall and studied the horizon of the basement and tried to ignore the hunger clawing at her belly.

She told herself she was staying still to conserve her limited physical resources. Already the waistband on her pants felt loose. She was losing weight. Probably dehydration. Staying put made sense. Why waste energy chasing down Amelia now? Nobody was waiting for her to save them.

Sure, there were other factors at work. She knew that.

She was too depressed to move.

And besides, there was nowhere to go.

Tate picked at the hem of her frayed jeans and waited for something to happen.

(CHAPTER THREE)

WHY WAS SHE STILL ALIVE?

Yago was coming.

Tate watched him approach slowly, her eyes narrowed down to slits. A tiny dot on the horizon, but definitely Yago. She could make out the white shirt, greenish hair. She recognized his stride. Easy and careful and menacing all at once.

He was alone. Interesting.

Tate dozed. When she woke, Yago was closer. She could see he didn't look too good. His head was too small — no, his neck was too big. Also interesting. A puzzle. She'd always liked doing puzzles.

Another stretch of time passed. Yago continued walking toward her, and now Tate could see the bruises stretching from his collarbone up over his chin. "Couldn't have happened to a nicer guy," Tate said out loud. She was surprised to hear how raspy her own voice sounded. How long had she gone without water? She had no way of counting time. A day? Two?

Tate amused herself watching Yago. She didn't move. Not even when one of his cruddy-looking sneakers touched her knee.

"Come with me," Yago said. He spoke in a half-dead monotone. He was missing a patch of hair over his right ear. As Tate watched, his hand went up automatically. He yanked a few greenish-brown hairs out by their roots and let them drift to the floor. This was not a sign of mental health.

"What happened to your throat?"

"Come on," Yago repeated dully.

"Amelia do that?" Tate could see the fléchette gun sticking out of the pocket of Yago's jeans. She wondered why he hadn't drawn it. Maybe he'd forgotten he had it. He looked as if he hadn't slept in a week.

"I said, *come on.*"

"No."

"No?"

"I'm not going anywhere with you," Tate said calmly. "I like it —"

Yago leaned over and moved his face toward hers until their noses were nearly touching. Stared into her eyes.

Then, with one fluid movement, Yago grabbed her arm and started pulling her up. He grunted, yanking Tate up onto her knees. Now he was starting to tick her off.

She tried to give him a shove. The effort sent her stumbling. Her knees buckled. She was weak. Her legs wouldn't support her. She fell awkwardly onto one knee.

Yago snarled like a rabid dog. He pulled out the fléchette gun.

Tate put up her hands. She halfheartedly tried to reach whatever it was inside her that turned her into the Mouth. From somewhere in her memory came the sound of a link ringing, ringing, ringing . . .

Something connected with her skull. She saw a burst of red light and then nothing.

A secretive *shush-shushing*. Tate's brain played pictures for her, trying to make sense of the sound. . . .

She was in study hall with her heavy chemistry textbook on her knees. Yvonne Flattery and Susan Nichols were whispering in the row behind her —
Shush-shush . . .

She was moving cautiously through a Rider swamp, the wind whistling through the weird bending trees —

Shush-shush . . .

She was on a camping trip with the Camp Fire Girls. She could see herself sleeping peacefully, a fire dancing around the brave circle of tents. The fire spreading slowly through the dry grasses until her nylon tent went up with a soft *woof*! Her sleeping bag was aflame, and her arm —

Her arm was on fire!

Tate's eyes popped open and she found herself lying on her back, watching the glassy ceiling of the basement pass overhead. Yago was dragging her across the basement by her arm. The shushing sounds were her clothes dragging over the floor.

"Stop," she muttered feebly. Then, louder, more urgently — "*Stop!*"

Yago stopped. He let go of her. Tate rolled into a fetal position and lay there feeling miserable.

Why was she still alive? Why didn't Yago just get rid of her? Tate turned her face to the ground and groaned.

Yago nudged her with his shoe. "Come on. Let's go."

"Go where?" Tate mumbled.

"Amelia wants to — see you."

"Oh — so now you're Amelia's assistant or something?"

"No!"

Yago's voice. There was something wrong about it. His usual arrogant tone was gone. His lofty messianic tones were gone. He sounded — scared.

Tate opened her eyes and looked up at Yago.

"Come on," Yago repeated.

Tate got to her knees and pulled herself shakily to her feet. She actually wanted to see Amelia now. Yago was pathetic. But maybe Amelia — well, maybe Amelia would help her draw this little drama to an end somehow. Tate didn't have the energy to hope for a happy ending.

"Which way?" Tate asked.

"Upstairs," Yago said. His expression was hard to read. Tate thought she saw something like relief mingling with wariness.

She took a step toward the elevator before she realized what Yago was telling her. Her guilt and inadequacy welled up. "Amelia is upstairs? I think — I was looking for her down here. Isn't she controlling the ship from one of the pits?"

Yago shook his head no and gestured with his chin toward the elevator. They walked single file with Tate in the lead. Yago was silent — no wisecracks, no self-aggrandizing remarks. *Geez*, Tate thought, *maybe whatever Amelia was doing to him wasn't so bad. . . .*

The elevator moved silently upward, and seconds later they were walking out under the towering arches into the alien hallway. Tate stepped forward cautiously — half-expecting Amelia or Charlie to jump out and tackle her. Nothing. The place felt as deserted as the basement.

Tate relaxed for a moment — and then the smell hit her. It was a humid, salty smell. The smell of growing things — like the sea at low tide.

Tate felt the fear welling up in her belly. Adrenaline pumped into her veins. She looked around wildly, trying to locate the origin of the smell.

Yago stood a few steps behind her, grinning and then laughing at her. Laughing at her sudden fear. She felt like smacking him. Yelling at him to shut up.

Because she *was* afraid. Somehow, intuitively, she knew this smell was bad. That earthy organic smell didn't belong on this cold dead ship.

Then the sounds filtered into her consciousness. She didn't know how she had missed them at first. Moist sounds that went on and on. They sounded — greedy. Like a baby sucking his soggy thumb or a derrick pulling oil from the ground.

"What is that?" Tate whispered.

"Go onto the bridge," Yago said. "See for yourself."

Tate hesitated.

She didn't want to get closer to that smell, that sound. But — she couldn't run away. She knew she would eventually come face-to-face with whatever was on the bridge. She preferred to face it on her feet. Delay would only make her weaker, more afraid.

Tate pushed down her fear. She took a step forward. And then another. She had to go fast or not at all. Yago stayed right behind her, making sure she went through the doorway onto the bridge and then blocking her way out. Tate wasn't sure what she was expecting but it wasn't —

Webs.

The machinery, the computers, the clean architecture of the bridge — it had all been covered by webs.

Something like spiderwebs.

But no, that wasn't quite right. These were webs but they weren't clean and precisely built like the webs of spiders. No — these were more like dirty cotton candy. Ugly, dirty swatches of grayish fuzz that made Tate long for a big can of Raid. She remembered a sweet old lady from her neighborhood trying to spray the gypsy moth nests that appeared in the trees around their apartment buildings.

You'd need an awful lot of Raid to take out these webs. They were huge — dirty wrappings stretching from the towering supporting struts all the way down to the chairs just a few feet from where Tate stood.

Tate's gaze darted to three lumpish masses inside the webs. They were writhing, squirming. Vaguely human forms. Amelia. Charlie. Duncan.

So.

This was their evolution.

This was how the Troika had achieved their "advanced forms." Tate could almost pity them. They were nothing but bugs. It was almost — sad.

But then — then her eye caught on a fourth lump, smaller than the others and covered in some sort of white goo — and her sadness turned to disgust. She could just make out a familiar jointed shape. It was the leg of a Rider. The leg was about all that was left.

Tate took a fast step back and whacked into Yago. He stood firmly in the doorway, blocking her escape.

"Why — why did you bring me here?" Tate asked, now cold with fear.

"Cells," Yago said bitterly. "As it turns out, living cells are the Troika's favorite snack food. I guess their big transformation is giving them the munchies, and since all of the Meanies and Riders are gone, you're going to be recycled. Sorry, but them's the breaks."

Tate let a beat pass as she absorbed this bizarre explanation. Had Yago finally slipped into true madness?

No, no — the evidence was here! The Troika wanted to — they wanted to devour her like they'd eaten that Rider. No. Please, no —

While Tate's brain skipped, Yago moved swiftly behind her and grabbed her by the wrists. Tate sensed a movement above her — inside the web.

No!

She didn't want to die like a fly caught in a spiderweb.

How could Yago do this to me? Tate thought wildly. *How could he do it to any living being?*

He was Evil.

He was Betrayal.

Tate felt barely like herself.

Something was happening. She was seeing in red, everything in red. And brighter than everything else, the Enemy. . . .

She/It surged forward.

It was big and powerful.

It was tongue. It was teeth. It was warm and wet and it stank of use.

The Mouth.

It closed over the head of the Enemy and it thought, *Now this evil will go away.*

(CHAPTER FOUR)

"HOW LONG BEFORE THEY — HATCH?"

Tate stumbled, shakily caught her balance. Through a pinkish mist she could see the towering door to the bridge. She was still alive. Yago hadn't gotten her yet, hadn't trapped her in the webs. . . .

Where was Yago? On the ground were nothing but a slick pool of slime.

Tate's head swam. She half-walked, half-crawled into the hallway, desperate to make sense of what had just happened.

Okay.

She had gone Mouth. That much was clear. She remembered the blood-colored vision from her last — episode.

But . . . but had she really ingested Yago? The last time she'd just sort of *nibbled* on him. But the last time, Jobs and 2Face and Anamull had come to

Yago's rescue. *This* time they weren't around to do the job.

Tate noticed — well, she wasn't hungry anymore.

And . . . and — then there was the foul taste in her mouth.

Tate's stomach heaved. She tried to hold it down, frightened of what she would see come up. But — no use. Her stomach cramped and she was powerless to stop it.

She squeezed her eyes tightly closed and felt her way down the hallway. She wouldn't look, nobody could make her look. . . .

<<You're pathetic.>>

Yago's voice. Ringing in her head.

Tate froze. She quickly scanned the hallway.

Empty.

Tate whimpered. "Yago is dead," she told herself shakily. "He can't hurt you. He can't talk —"

<<Not so fast. It looks like we have a little plot twist on our hands.>>

Tate covered her ears.

She turned to run down the hallway, back toward the elevator.

<<Where are we going?>> came Yago's voice.

"We're — we're not going anywhere!" Tate screamed. "Go away — leave me alone!" Her voice was high with hysteria.

<<Hey, what kind of attitude is that? I didn't *ask* you to go Mouth or whatever, you know. The least you can do now is to behave civilly. In fact, I think you owe me an apology.>>

Tate made fists of her hands and stomped her feet like a toddler having a temper tantrum.

<<Oh, that's very mature. That's going to solve everything.>>

Tate stopped and did a slow circle. She couldn't flee Yago's voice. Yago was somehow inside her. Either that, or she was going completely mad.

<<Hey, you know, you have very good eyesight. What is it? 20/20? You go under the knife, or are you just naturally blessed?>>

Yago could see out of her eyes? Tate blinked slowly and rubbed her eyes. She — she didn't know how she felt about that. She — she would think about that later.

What she needed now was to put her head down somewhere. No, to actually lie down and take a little nap. Tate sat down against the wall of the corridor and stretched out. She was so sleepy. . . .

<<Hey! Hey, what are you doing? I'm not tired! What are you? An oversized snake sleeping off a meal?>>

Yago's taunts continued, but Tate drifted off.

Tate dreamed.

She was flying through space, Earth spread out below her like a great gray marble. She could see the Dark Zone, the Light Zone, the strange misshapen lumps that had come from the impact with the Rock.

Then something happened.

Something began to spread over the gray like mold. Tate experienced a moment of fear — what was this new assault on Earth? Then she realized the something was green.

Plants, Tate thought luxuriously, knowing she was dreaming and enjoying the dream. She watched until all of the gray patches were covered and the gray marble had become a soft fuzzy sphere.

Her vision zoomed in.

Now she was walking through a garden, surrounded by apple trees and grass green enough for a golf course. A gentle breeze rippled though a clump of orange daylilies and Queen Anne's lace.

She put out one hand and ran it through the leaves of a bush growing along the pathway. Soft.

Children were playing hide-and-seek. She could hear their high-pitched squeals of laughter. Her attention was drawn to a little girl with brown hair and Jobs's distracted brown eyes.

Jobs's daughter.

Somehow she knew the little girl's name was Tate.

Then the garden was gone and Billy was standing before her. With a strangely distant smile, a benevolent smile, he reached out and handed her something.

Tate looked down. It was a birthday card. The front of the card showed a pink cake topped with blazing candles. Tate could see her own brown hands opening the card.

Inside it read: *Three elements: The Source, the five embodied in me, and —*

The dream-Billy abruptly screamed, his voice sounding like a siren. "Wake up! Wake up!"

Tate sat up fast and felt her dreamworld spin away. The lovely garden was gone. She was back on Mother. With a very nasty taste in her mouth.

The overwhelming sleepiness was gone, but she

still felt sluggish. Her head was pounding, she couldn't quite catch her breath, and — and her arms and legs were twitching uncontrollably.

What now? Tate wondered wearily. Was she having a spasm? A seizure?

Tate's right arm violently jerked up in the air like a puppet's and then fell limply at her side.

<<Move!>>

A puppet . . .

Yago! Yago was trying to control her body!

Terrified, Tate watched her hand jerk a few inches to the left. She thought of the Baby, the eyeless horror that had controlled Tamara. Poor Tamara . . . it'd been a long time since Tate had even had a moment to think about her. Hard to grieve on the go.

Tate's hand twitched again. Angrily, she crossed her arms, pinning her hands under her armpits.

"Stop it, Yago!" she said shortly, aware of how ridiculous she would look if anyone could see her. The simple act of talking made her breathless. "Go ahead and — and haunt me if you must but have some respect for my body. Please."

<<Oh, beautiful. Moral platitudes from a girl who eats people.>>

Tate felt deeply uneasy talking to a voice in her

head. She had enough problems without dealing with — with schizophrenia. Or whatever this was. She had to figure out what was going on. Maybe she could hear Yago's voice because she felt bad about what the Mouth had done to him. . . .

"Just — just quit it, okay?" she whispered edgily.

<<Or what?>> Yago challenged bitterly. <<What more can you do to me now?>>

"Hurt myself," Tate said immediately.

<<You're not serious.>>

"Try me."

There was a pause. A long one. Long enough for Tate to hope Yago was gone for good. But then —

<<Fine, you drive,>> Yago said. <<But if you don't mind, may I suggest we hit the road? The Troika has plans for your sweet little cells, remember?>>

"I'm not sure I can walk," Tate said.

<<Then crawl.>>

With effort, Tate fell forward onto her hands and knees. She forced herself to move a leg, the opposite arm. Blood pounded in her veins. She moved a few inches toward the elevator. Then a few more. The pain in her head made her nauseous. She gagged, paused for a deep breath, moved forward again.

<<Could you pick it up?>> Yago seemed unaffected by her physical distress. <<Not to be rude, but I feel the need for speed.>>

"How long before they — hatch?" Tate gasped.

<<No idea.>>

Another few inches. Tate had crawled a few feet now. The elevator looked slightly closer.

"Can they — grow — without more cells?" Tate asked.

<<Don't fool yourself into thinking we can starve them out,>> Yago said forcefully. <<They'll still grow, they'll still hatch. Only they'll be angrier when they do. Hungrier. More eager to kill us.>>

"How do you know?"

<<How do you know I don't!>>

Tate had to admit Yago had been right to get her moving. Maybe he was right about the Troika, too. Maybe she would be wise to trust him — at least a little bit.

She crawled up to the elevator and pulled herself into a shaky stand.

<<What are you waiting for?>> Yago demanded. <<We'll be safer in the basement.>>

"I'm — I'm thinking maybe we should get rid of the Troika now," Tate said. "While they're helpless in those webs. If we could find some sort of weapon or make a fire —"

<<Attacking them is suicide,>> Yago said.

"How do you know?"

<<They're not helpless,>> Yago insisted. <<At least Amelia isn't. She'll know if we try to attack her. She'll know. And she'll kill us.>>

Tate tried to think. Yago was a coward. That much had been clear from the day they'd all gathered at Cape Canaveral, back before the Rock hit. And she didn't see what good it would do to hide away in the basement. Amelia would find them eventually. And, even if Amelia wasn't helpless now, she was bound to be stronger after she hatched.

They needed a plan.

Now.

(CHAPTER FIVE)

"I'M HERE, MOTHER."

To keep Yago quiet, to buy time, Tate stepped into the elevator and took a too-fast ride down to the basement. The air was much clearer there. Tate could think again.

Thanks, Yago, she thought. He was pretty good at looking out for her skin now that her skin was his skin, too. Honestly, she felt pretty good. Her hunger was completely gone. Because — because she'd just had such a big meal. The thought made Tate's head spin. She would stop thinking about it. She had to.

The plan.

Forget this situation with Yago.

Think about what to do next.

Tate started to slowly walk across the basement.

What if she went Mouth? Could she destroy the Troika? Dicey. The mutation was too unpredictable.

What if it didn't appear when she needed it? They needed a more reliable weapon.

"What happened to your gun?" Tate asked out loud.

<<You ate it,>> Yago said, sounding oddly amused. <<Why? What are you thinking?>>

"Nothing . . ."

<<We need to hide, Tate. Not plan an attack on Amelia.>>

"Fine. Okay."

Maybe Yago is right, Tate told herself. Maybe fighting the Troika was pointless. But hiding was pointless, too.

<<You're awfully quiet all of a sudden,>> Yago said suspiciously. <<What are you thinking about?>>

"Nothing. Just trying to decide where we should hide."

<<Don't lie to me, Tate. Thanks to you, I'm stuck in your body. Don't you think I deserve to know what you're thinking? Don't you think I deserve to vote on our next move?>>

Well, no. But it wasn't as if Tate could keep a secret from Yago for long. "I'm thinking we should — toss in the towel. Leave the Troika to their destiny."

<<What kind of coward are you?>> Yago repeated derisively.

"Yago," Tate said wearily. "Calling me names isn't going to make a big impression at this point."

<<Five minutes ago you wanted to play the hero and stop the Troika,>> Yago said irritably. <<Now you want to lie down and play dead. Excuse me for being confused!>>

Tate knew Yago was setting her up. Stop the Troika from doing what? She didn't want to take the bait, but — "What is Amelia planning?" she asked reluctantly.

<<All I know is that Duncan programmed Mother to go — somewhere specific,>> Yago said. <<A planet.>>

"So?"

<<So — I got the distinct impression that whatever — whoever — was living on that planet wouldn't be celebrating Amelia Day anytime soon.>>

"More recycling?"

<<Good guess.>>

This news deeply depressed Tate. She didn't want to play the hero. She just wanted to — rest. Give up. Obviously, on the off chance that Yago was telling the truth, that wasn't happening. She couldn't die and leave the Troika cruising the universe. Who knew what kind of trouble they'd cause?

"We could breach the hull somehow," Tate said. "Let the atmosphere out."

<<With no weapons? No tools? Oh, I'm forgetting. You could just gnaw your way through.>>

Tate stopped walking.

The answer was right in front of her. Okay, not *right* in front of her. It was off to the left and about two hundred yards away. Close enough. A pit fitted out with several oddly proportioned chairs. Chairs where the aliens who had built this ship sat and connected with their über-computer.

Alberto had been the first among the Remnants to discover what the chairs really were. He'd been the first to hear Mother's voice.

Back on Earth before the Rock, Alberto had been an engineer. He'd designed the solar sails on the *Mayflower*. He was a brilliant man and one with enough political savvy to get himself and his son two seats on the only ride off the doomed planet.

Connecting with Mother had driven him mad. He didn't live for long after that.

Yago'd had a go in the chair next. He'd been arrogant enough to think it would be no big deal. He'd barely survived. But, since then, he'd had long periods when he insisted he was like a god, alternating with periods when he seemed to forget his divine status.

Only Billy had been Mother's match. And Billy — Billy was not entirely human. He was something — more.

Tate was no Billy.

She was no Alberto even.

But — but . . . if she could somehow connect with Mother and control her — then she could do anything. She could destroy Amelia and Duncan and Charlie and go back to Earth just to make sure her friends weren't waiting for her.

And — if it didn't work, she would end up like Alberto . . . completely insane.

Having so little to hold her back made her bold.

But she was still afraid.

"Do it fast," Tate whispered to herself.

Yago immediately figured out what she had in mind. He'd seen her looking toward the not-too-distant pit. He might be in a slightly weird situation, but he wasn't stupid.

<<No!>> he said forcefully. <<Oh, god, please — no!>> Tate had never heard Yago's voice so lacking in posturing or artifice. He sounded completely and honestly terrified.

"Shut up," she said tonelessly. She walked quickly toward the pit, ignoring the steady stream of begging that Yago was letting loose. She hopped down into the pit and approached one of the chairs.

<<Tate — Tate, please! Let's talk about this. I — I've been there. You don't know what you're doing.>>

"I wonder which chair is a good one," Tate mused out loud. "Some of the connections to Mother are broken, aren't they?"

<<Tate, listen. Please. Mother can do — terrible things. She can   she can read thoughts you never even knew you had. Access nightmares from when you were a baby. She'll learn what scares you the most and use it against you. Tate — don't. I'm — I'm scared. I can't live through that again.>>

Tate ignored Yago's pleas. She cautiously approached the closest chair and gingerly lowered herself into it. *Maybe it won't be so bad,* she told herself shakily.

<<Get up!>> Yago screamed hysterically. <<Quick. There's still time. . . .>>

"I'm here, Mother," Tate whispered, her voice hoarse with fear. "Let's you and I have a little chat, shall we?"

Tate braced herself for Mother's reaction.

47

Nothing. Tate might as well have been back in L.A., sitting in her grandfather's La-Z-Boy.

<<Get up,>> Yago pleaded tensely.

Tate's body twitched with nerves. The silence stretched on. She began thinking about Alberto. About the way he'd drooled and babbled.

"Maybe — maybe this isn't such a good idea. . . ." Tate tried to get up and found her muscles wouldn't move.

Yago began to whimper low. <<She won't let you go,>> he said. <<Not until she's finished with you.>>

There came a sudden noise — like a freight train in the distance, coming closer fast. The sound grew in intensity until it blossomed into a screaming wail that threatened to burst Tate's eardrums.

Tate felt something like a pinprick in her head. She tried to relax, tried to show Mother she was a friend by thinking friendly thoughts, but — the sensation was growing in force, setting her teeth on edge.

Mother was poking at her brain. This — this wasn't what she'd imagined. She'd expected a deluge of data. She'd expected — it was hard to explain, the presence of a rational consciousness. She'd expected to somehow have a conversation with Mother. Bargain with her. Negotiate.

But Mother didn't seem rational. She wasn't efficiently accessing Tate's memories — she was banging around like a tired child having a screaming fit in a filing cabinet.

Brutal scenes flicked to life for a split second — a bloody battlefield strewn with dead Riders, Amelia disintegrating into a puddle of decay — before Mother tossed them aside.

<<This isn't good,>> Yago said. <<I think Mother is angry.>>

Different scenes now. More personal. Lasting longer.

Tate's mother weeping at her mother's funeral.

A small, scabby-kneed Tate hugging a lamppost as Jennifer Taylor Smith's parents packed their meager belongings into a U-Haul.

A goldfish floating belly up in a slimy-looking bowl.

Tate got the message: grief, loss, abandonment. Billy. Mother missed Billy. Tate understood. She hoped Mother knew she was innocent — she had done nothing to take Billy away from her.

But Mother wasn't into subtlety.

Or perhaps she just didn't like suffering alone.

She did something to Tate's body and suddenly Tate was overwhelmed by a sadness that was like a wet cloth dragging down on her head. She dwelled on all she had lost to the Rock: her home, her family, her dog. Poor innocent Lily. She'd never hurt anyone.

She was powerless to control the sobs racking her body. Yago was weeping, too. A pitiful sound.

The grief finally drained away.

Mother toyed with Tate's mind. Called up another emotion.

Anger.

Now the adrenaline pumping through Tate's veins was accompanied by images of all the bullies who'd made her long life miserable — playground bullies whose names she had forgotten, the Meanies, 2Face, Yago. How she hated them! Rage consumed her until —

It was replaced.

Replaced with pain.

(CHAPTER SIX)

TIME CEASED TO EXIST.

Mother knew pain. She enjoyed pain, appreciated it. She slowed her frantic march through Tate's emotions, seemingly having found a theme she wished to dwell on.

She dredged up memories from Tate's mind one by one, turning them over, examining them carefully, playing them out in lavish detail. They say the human mind cannot remember pain. Tate was sad to learn this was apparently not true —

Bright lights. The orthodontist who smelled strongly of mouthwash tightened Tate's braces. Twist, twist, twist with his glittering metallic instrument — until Tate could feel the roots of her teeth all the way up into her sinuses. Until the weight of her tongue resting against her bottom front teeth was enough to make her weep and she was scared to close her mouth —

High-pitched giggles and a huge pink-and-white object rushing toward her face. Tate had just enough time to identify it as her little cousin Gaby's pink Stride Rite sandal before it smashed into her nose with enough force to send blood fountaining, her nose instantly ballooning, the pain making her whimper. It had been an accident. But it had hurt.

The gravel-covered ground came rushing up as she flew over her twenty-speed's handlebars and landed awkwardly on her side. An audible *snap* as her forearm splintered.

Why?

Was Mother sending her a message?

Tate may never have puzzled it out on her own. Not under these circumstances. But Mother seemed to feel her question. She wanted Tate to understand.

The pain drained out of Tate's body. She went limp as Mother put an image into her mind. An image of Duncan doing something behind a flipped-up control panel. The image meant nothing to Tate — she wasn't even sure if it was real or meant to be a metaphor for something — but Mother made sure she got the message.

Duncan had infected Mother with a virus designed to degrade her into a simpler, easier-to-control operating system.

He'd given her a lobotomy.

Mother was mad. And she was going to make Tate pay because Tate was the only one left.

Time ceased to exist.

Tate lost herself.

She forgot Yago.

Days passed while Tate sat frozen in that chair. Or years. Or perhaps it all flashed by in seconds. It didn't matter. It was an eternity.

Mother raged as Duncan's virus slowly consumed her. She mourned the loss of every memory. She reached for skills she no longer possessed — and struck out with anger when she found them gone.

Mother fought for survival.

Her assault of brutal images and emotions didn't stop. Maybe it was a steam valve for Mother's anger. Maybe she was distracted by the virus and forgot to stop punishing them. Tate didn't know. She stopped caring.

It went on and on.

Time passed.

Until, finally, long after Tate had stopped hoping, stopped caring, some critical juncture was reached.

Mother began to recede. To become something —

lesser. The images played before Tate's eyes lost their edge. The pain in her muscles dulled. She found she could move her right pinky finger — and then her whole arm.

<<Get up.>>

Tate didn't recognize the voice in her head at first. Then she remembered. Yago. Right. With a gigantic effort, she heaved her body up out of the chair. Her knees crumpled. She landed in a pile on the floor.

She felt bad. Very bad. She couldn't catch her breath. Her head was pounding. She was tired. She was confused. She had to — what? Do something . . .

<<Tate! The elevator!>>

Tate lifted her head to look. The enormous pyramidal structure of the elevator was covered in dirty webs. Tate squinted with effort. "It's okay," she whispered weakly. "I don't see them. They're not in the webs."

She remembered now. Amelia, Charlie, Duncan. They were turning into huge bugs. Or something. They wanted to — recycle her cells.

<<That's what worries me. Tate, look. Do you see?>>

Tate forced herself to focus more carefully on

the webs; she willed her mind to work. She could see a tattered hole. Tate got painfully to her feet. She took a few cautious steps closer. Beneath the hole in the web there was a trail. Something like the slimy trail snails leave behind — only this trail was smoking. Like a trail of acid.

<<Do you see them?>> Yago demanded. <<Don't just stand there, look for them!>>

Tate turned in a slow circle, the hairs rising on the back of her head. "Where is the Troika?" she whispered.

<<Or, more to the point, *what* Is the Troika?>> Yago asked.

"I — I'm not sure, but I think they went that-away."

<<Then I vote we go the other way.>>

And then Tate was running, trying to run. Fleeing. Panicked.

<<Get somewhere we can put our back against the wall,>> Yago encouraged her. <<We need to see what's coming.>>

Tate's ill-used body was clumsy. She stumbled at first. But fear helped her coordination. Soon she was flying across the basement, heading toward the same spot on the wall where Yago had found her.

Maybe. She thought she was heading that way, but it was difficult to tell. There weren't enough landmarks.

Her footsteps echoed in the eerily empty ship.

Her eyes strained for some sign of trouble.

Nothing, nothing — the slime trail didn't go this way. That meant they were safe. It had to mean the Troika was somewhere else.

Only . . .

Something was wrong.

"Do you smell that?" Tate panted.

<<Thanks to you and your big mouth, I have no — yes. Yes, I smell something like . . . matches.>>

"Something burning." Tate slowed down, her heart thumping painfully.

She looked up.

(CHAPTER SEVEN)

<<NOBODY EVER SAID EVOLUTION WAS PRETTY.>>

The transparent ceiling above Tate's head glistened wetly.

"What the —"

Tate's mind whirled, collecting data. The smell was stronger now. Something like smoldering plastic. She studied the weird stuff for another long moment. Had one of the Troika left this stuff behind? Had they turned into giant slugs? Then — a flash of movement . . .

She bolted!

<<Where are we going?>>

Tate didn't bother to answer. She just wanted to get away. She'd run only another few yards when something dropped on her head. A searing pain. The smell of burning hair. Tate beat at the spot with her hands, desperate to get whatever it was off her. Her hair was on fire!

Another drop fell.

This one hit her shoe. She watched the nylon smoke, felt a dull pain on the top of her foot.

She made a fast move to the left.

Another drop.

It hit her shoe precisely on top of the hole left by the last one. The pain on her foot increased tenfold. Smoke was rising from the perfectly circular hole in her shoe.

"Stop it!" she yelled hysterically. Why did the drops keep hitting her? Were they aiming for her?

Tate laughed nervously. She was getting paranoid.

Off in front of her a spattering of drops fell. She relaxed a bit. Those had missed her. They *weren't* aiming for her. But then Tate got closer and saw the drops formed a pattern on the floor. They formed . . . letters.

She could just make them out. They said —
WE'RE GOING TO GET YOU.

Tate stifled a scream. "That's the Troika. That, that slime."

<<Nobody ever said evolution was pretty.>>

She turned left, right — unsure of what to do next. "Yago, help me. . . ." she whimpered.

<<Watch out!>>

A great glob of the stuff was dripping off the ceiling. It fell to the floor and began to move sinuously to form a circle around Tate. The floor smoked wherever the slime touched it. The smell was acrid, awful. The pain in Tate's head and on her foot was intensifying. If that big glob touched her —

<<Tate — run!>> Yago screamed. <<Go, go, go!>>

Tate turned 360 degrees, whimpering. She was surrounded. "I can't go through that stuff," she whispered. "I'll get burned."

<<That's better than being trapped here!>>

No. Not to Tate it wasn't. The pain in her foot was unbelievable. She couldn't live with those burns all over her body. No, she was staying right where she was.

Inside her head, Yago began to scream.

Amelia knew she should hurry.

Tate was the only living thing left on the ship — who knew where that rat Yago had gotten to? — and she wanted to recycle her before Charlie and Duncan finished programming Mother and came looking for her.

Amelia calculated she had only .000072 marks before they finished. Not much time.

Still . . . she hesitated.

Maybe that wasn't so odd. Tate was to be her last meal during the long voyage to Attbi that lay ahead. More than 340 million light-years. Even with Mother's excellent navigation system and powerful engines, it would be a long fast. What was so odd about taking a few moments to savor the anticipation of her last meal?

Only — Amelia found this difficult to admit but her new incarnation didn't allow for any self-delusion — that wasn't the only reason she was hesitating.

She couldn't ignore the fact that Tate very well might be the last human alive. Surely the ones abandoned on the planet had perished of thirst by now. And Yago — well, Amelia's suspicion was that Charlie had hunted him down against her orders. The Troika itself certainly couldn't be considered human anymore.

That left Tate. The last of the home team, Amelia's team. A wave of nostalgia hit Amelia hard — being human had been *wonderful*. They were the best species *ever*.

Whoa. Amelia fought to get a grip. In this new form, her emotions were oversized, difficult to control, engulfing. She was going to have to be careful.

Time for that snack. Amelia made herself into a smaller circle, drawing frightened wails from Tate. Tate drew herself in, made herself small. Hands to her chest, head tucked down. It was pitiful.

Amelia slowly widened the circle again. Maybe she should keep Tate alive. Something to remind her of where she came from. She could heal up the burn wounds on her head, her foot. Charlie could build a cage. Mother could synthesize some food and water. Pizza maybe . . .

Bad idea, Amelia decided swiftly. Having Tate around would be too depressing. Amelia couldn't lie to herself — even if she wanted to — she'd be jealous if Tate were around.

Humans were just better-looking than . . . whatever it was Amelia had become.

Of course, Amelia was superior. Smarter. More evolved. She could change forms at will. She didn't have to look like a puddle of snot if she didn't want to. She could look like a model, if she wanted to. She just needed to learn how to control her cells. All she needed was practice.

So practice, Amelia told herself, making herself ignore the disgust she felt. She twisted her cells, forcing them to take on the form of Tate's face.

Oh, Tate's reaction was hilarious! She was so

surprised, so — horrified. Just for kicks, Amelia mimicked her scared look — mouth open, eyes wide.

Tate turned away. Hid her face.

That wouldn't do! A wave of anger engulfed Amelia. She twisted her cells again so they now resembled a hand. She reached out and touched Tate's cheek.

Tate screamed.

An angry red welt was forming on Tate's cheek. Ouch. Looked painful.

Amelia was overcome by remorse. She hadn't meant to hurt Tate, she thought bitterly as she dropped back into the form of a circle. She wasn't a *monster*.

Or was she?

I am a monster, Amelia thought sadly. *I'm — I'm ugly.* Smart was nice as far as it went — but Amelia wanted to be beautiful again. She wanted to be *human* again. She wanted hair and teeth and arms and legs.

Oh, well. Amelia was too smart, too evolved to waste time wishing for something she could never have. She'd spent enough time feeling sorry for herself. Once she ate Tate, she could forget about humans. It would be as if they'd never existed.

Amelia constricted the circle.

She tried to ignore Tate's reaction. She wanted to close her eyes — but she no longer had eyes to close. Data streamed into her brain from a million receptors.

Tate screamed. She made a clumsy attempt to jump over the circle Amelia had formed. Tate's legs twitched. She yanked herself back into the middle of the circle. "Stop it!" she yelled. "I'm not going through that, that *slime!*" Tate's legs twitched oddly — as if she were possessed.

Or —

Maybe not possessed.

Amelia's curiosity was even bigger than her hunger.

"Yago, quit!" Tate yelled.

Amelia understood now. Yago was somehow living inside Tate. Even more interesting, he seemed to have some control over her body.

Tate was the Mouth.

Yes. It made sense. Yago had gone to fetch Tate for recycling and she'd devoured him. That's why he'd suddenly disappeared. Only he wasn't really dead. He was alive somehow inside Tate.

Amelia was struck by a sudden, wonderful, desperate idea.

She had to get Tate.

If that fool Yago could gain some control over Tate's body, Amelia figured she should have no trouble taking over entirely. She would be human again. She wouldn't have to be a monster anymore.

(CHAPTER EIGHT)

<<THEY'RE COMING AFTER US.>>

Go Mouth, Amelia silently urged Tate.

She waited. But Tate just stood in the center of the Amelia-circle, protectively cradling her burned cheek and letting out pitiful little pain noises.

Encouragement, Amelia decided. *That's what she needs.*

Amelia turned into a sword shape and poked at Tate's belly, being careful not to get close enough to burn her.

Tate shrank away. No Mouth.

Amelia stretched herself out very thin, forming a shallow lake that covered the floor all around Tate. Now Tate couldn't move an inch without burning her feet.

Tate froze in horror and murmured something too low for Amelia to hear. No Mouth.

The new Amelia was not a patient creature. She

wanted to lash out at Tate, punish her for resisting — but no, that wouldn't do. She needed Tate's body intact. She would just have to control her aggravation and think the problem through.

Maybe Tate just didn't *want* to eat a disgusting ball of slime. Amelia quickly dismissed the thought as unproductive. If that was the case, all bets were off.

Maybe . . . maybe it was just that she wasn't in a form Tate could easily get her mouth around. Amelia drew herself in as tightly as possible and formed an oversized ball. She hoped she didn't look like a huge booger.

Tate hesitated and then fled, moving away from Amelia and the elevator.

"Why are you letting her get away?"

Duncan announced his arrival rudely. Amelia didn't like his tone. Perhaps hunger was making him grouchy.

"Oh, hello," Amelia replied, smoothly hiding her irritation.

She could see him oozing along the ceiling. A wave of repulsion hit her. Is that what she looked like now? Unbearable.

She allowed herself to picture the human Duncan. Brains hidden behind movie-star eyes.

"The journey to Attbi is long," Amelia said

sweetly. "*I thought we should savor our last meal. I was just waiting for you to get here.*"

Asking Duncan to delay a meal after the hungry work of transformation — it was a challenge. If Duncan's hunger was anything like Amelia's, he would have a difficult time mastering it. He'd be reluctant to share his meal with Amelia. And aware of the fact Charlie could arrive at any moment.

"Sure," Duncan said with impressive ease. "What do you have in mind?"

"A simple game of cat and mouse, a bit of exercise," Amelia said. "I'm still learning what this — beautiful new body can do."

"Yes," Duncan agreed. "Some experiments along those lines should make the trip to Attbi go much more quickly."

Oh, Duncan. He *was* special.

Amelia would miss him. But his attractiveness and intelligence were the problem exactly. Amelia had no desire to share Tate's body with anyone who could challenge her mastery. Duncan had to go.

She would use his arrogance against him. And quickly — before Charlie joined their little party.

"The game is to see how long we can make the hunt last," Amelia said. "To frighten her without hurting her. Points for creativity."

Duncan took off after the fleeing Tate. Amelia raced after him. If her plan was to work, she couldn't let him get too far ahead.

<<They're coming after us,>> Yago said suddenly. He could see only what Tate could see, but he was calmer and better able to interpret the data. <<Cut left!>>

Tate did what Yago told her. "What do you mean — they?" she asked breathlessly.

<<There are two. One on the floor. And one on the ceiling behind us and coming up fast!>> Yago yelled. <<Mr. Duncan, I presume? Or is that you, Charlie, you old dog?>>

Two of them? There was no way she could get away from two. *This is it,* Tate thought. *I'm about to die.* She was going to be . . . recycled. Like that Rider.

She was scared.

Maybe . . .

Maybe if she begged they would let her live.

On second thought, she wasn't dying like a wimp.

<<So, Tate — hungry?>>

"You think we — I — can eat these guys?" Tate asked.

<<Don't know,>> Yago said. <<Depends on

how you feel about oysters on the half shell. 'Cause you're looking at the mother of all slime picnics.>>

"I hate shellfish," Tate said.

<<Maybe it's time to rethink that,>> Yago said. <<Don't look now but Slime Monster Number Two is directly overhead.>>

Tate didn't look up. "Where's the other one?"

<<To the right — *and* in front of us. I think it's forming another circle. Go Mouth now!>>

"I can't — I don't know how. . . ." Tate stopped running. She wasn't sure if it was best to go forward or back or just stay where she was. "When I feel threatened, it just happens —"

<<Well, crack the code.>>

"I — I don't want to eat them," Tate managed to get out. "Who knows what I'd be letting into my head?"

<<I can handle a slime monster!>>

"You don't know that —"

Tate didn't have time to finish the thought.

Duncan — or whoever, whatever — began to drip off the ceiling as a fine mist. The tiny droplets fell on Tate's shoulders. On her head.

Tate saw a bright burst of flame. The smell of burning hair reached her nostrils.

"Ahh!" Tate batted at her hair. She shook her

head like a wet dog. The flames went out. But the mist was still falling.

<<Watch out!>>

Busy with her hair, Tate had stumbled into a thin layer of slime. Where had that come from? She froze in horror, looking down at her feet. Her rubber soles began to smoke and then melt into a whitish puddle. The heat leaped up around her ankles. The nylon upper began to melt.

<<There's no way out!>>

No way out . . .

Something was happening.

The red vision. The tongue. The teeth.

Tate tried to resist, tried to hold on, but she felt herself slip away. Then there was only the bright-hot ecstasy of teeth grinding together.

"*Whoa — ho — ho!*" Duncan laughed in Amelia's head. "*What have we here? Interesting, very interesting — so primitive. Primal, almost, wouldn't you say? Nothing like the mutation I had.*"

Tate's transformation wasn't as violent as Amelia had expected. Tate still sort of looked like Tate — only her head and mouth and teeth were bigger. Yes, the teeth were *much* bigger.

Up on the ceiling, Duncan was withdrawing,

pulling himself away from the gaping Mouth that was snapping at him like a rabid dog.

"*Lots of pieces,*" he advised Amelia. "*Get into lots of pieces so she can't get her teeth into you. Well, well, that was fun. I guess I finally bugged her enough — Amelia, what are you —*"

Amelia had formed herself into a ball once again. Now she zoomed past Duncan, heading straight for Tate's snapping jaws.

CHAPTER NINE

<<THREE'S A CROWD. MAN, THREE'S A THRONG.>>

The Mouth bit down on the Enemy. The Enemy was slippery. It slid down her throat almost eagerly. The Mouth gulped and gagged. Too much, too big . . . But the Enemy would not come up. The Mouth swallowed and . . . and . . .

Tate stumbled. She saw the floor. Smelled smoke.

<<Tate — you with us?>> Yago's voice.

"Sleep," Tate mumbled. "I need sleep."

<<Sleep now and we're all history.>> Not Yago's voice. Tate felt her head jerk up and her eyelids open wider. She hadn't moved them. Someone else was controlling them.

"Amelia?" Tate asked warily. She struggled for control of her body. Her eyes and head responded, but her feet began to twitch oddly. Her right foot — oh, agony. The pain was radiating up her bones into her legs. She did not want to move her foot. "Stop it!"

<<Duncan and Charlie are both out there. Duncan got scared and ran away for now. But their big goal in life is going to be eating this body. We have to stay awake and be ready to fight.>>

Definitely Amelia.

Tate moaned low. "I told you this would happen," she said.

<<I can control her.>> Yago said arrogantly.

Amelia laughed. <<You? You couldn't control a finger puppet. Now listen up. The best thing for all of us is for me to take control until this threat is past us. Then we can talk, figure out some form of — schedule.>>

"Schedule?" Tate said angrily. "You want to make a schedule for controlling my body? What are we going to do — tack it up on the fridge? Review it at our family meetings?"

The burst of anger kept her alert as long as she was talking, but as soon as she finished, she began to feel limp with fatigue. Sleep. She needed sleep. . . .

Tate sank cross-legged onto the floor and rested her head in her hands. Her foot was throbbing dully.

She was already nodding off when her eyelids moved slowly upward, offering her a view of her fingers.

<<No sleeping,>> Amelia said determinedly.

Tate didn't need to close her eyelids to fall asleep. Her eyes had already rolled back in her rather crowded head.

Tate dreamed.

She was floating above the gray Earth. She would have been at tree height had there been any trees. The landscape was nothing but dirt. Lifeless. A cemetery for her friends, and the seven billion who had died before them.

Such a sad place. Such a lonely place.

Then Tate's eyes picked up movement. She strained, trying to see what it was. Her vision shifted, she saw them — bands of people marching steadily toward some distant object. They were like believers moving toward Mecca. Or wildebeests converging on a water hole.

Primitive. Matted hair. They wore furs, bundles of shapeless clothing. They looked exhausted — shoulders hunched forward, eyes on the ground.

Tate scanned the horizon, trying to unlock the puzzle, anxious to see where they were going — but there was nothing on the horizon but dust.

Tate woke to the sound of arguing.

<<Believe me,>> Yago was saying, <<if I knew

how to wake her up, I'd do it. Anything to shut you up.>>

Sensations began to flood in. Her right foot was throbbing hotly. She avoided looking at it, imagining her burned skin.

Her neck ached. Someone was trying to turn it and succeeding only in making her twitch painfully. Amelia. Judging from the ache in her muscles, Amelia had been twitching them for hours.

"Cool it, Amelia," Tate said irritably.

<<I'm trying to see something other than the floor,>> Amelia said in a huffy tone. <<We could be ambushed at any second. I — you — we're smelling something strange. They're close.>>

<<Tate!>> Yago interrupted. <<I'm so glad you're awake.>>

"Why?" Tate asked warily. Her drowsiness was falling away and she was starting to feel scared again. Amelia was right. Two more slime monsters were still out there. She couldn't run on her foot. It felt as if someone had drilled a hole straight through it. If Duncan and Charlie attacked, she was toast.

<<You snooze and I'm locked up with this lunatic,>> Yago muttered. <<Alone.>>

<<Listen,>> Amelia interrupted. <<We've been discussing the situation while you were asleep and

we agree. When Charlie and Duncan put in an appearance, you can't go Mouth.>>

<<Three's a crowd,>> Yago put in. <<Man, three's a throng.>>

Tate agreed. Vehemently. But she didn't like Yago and Amelia giving her orders. "The Mouth just *appears*," she said peevishly. "I can't control it."

<<Then you have to let *me* do it,>> Amelia said.

Tate felt like telling Amelia where to go. But then she imagined another voice added to the chorus in her head. Psycho Charlie. Arrogant Duncan. Or — oh, god — maybe even *both* of them. Not a happy thought.

Then came the smell.

Matches. Sulfur. Something burning.

Faint now, but growing stronger.

<<Do you smell that?>> Yago asked urgently.

<<They're coming,>> Amelia said, and she sounded much calmer than Tate felt. <<Let go, Tate. Just — just relax and I'll take care of everything.>>

Tate didn't trust anyone who promised to take care of everything. Besides, she didn't know how to let go of her body. And, if she *could* do it, she wondered if she'd ever be able to wrest control back from Amelia.

She looked around. Was that a glistening patch

on the ceiling off to her left? Yes, she was quite certain it was. Duncan was up there. Or Charlie.

Tate's heart leaped up like a fluttering bird. She tried to run. The pain in her right foot brought her to her knees, whimpering.

<<Do it,>> Yago whispered conspiratorially. <<Amelia's our only chance. When this is all over — if we survive — I'll help you put her down.>>

<<I heard that,>> Amelia said flatly.

The glistening patch was growing closer now. The sulfur smell was stronger. Tate made her decision.

It wasn't difficult.

Tate wanted to hide. She let the feeling consume her. She imagined herself growing smaller, shrinking down to stand next to a bite-size Yago. She imagined Amelia rising up, swelling like one of those hot-air balloons in the Thanksgiving parade —

<<Hey!>> Tate yelled.

Amelia had sensed her opening. Tate felt Amelia hovering over her eagerly — and then Amelia was squeezing her, suffocating her, crushing her, pushing her roughly aside —

Tate was weightless. Gravity was gone.

It was like the floating moment before sleep descends. Her body felt fuzzy, distant. The pain in her foot had receded to a dull ache. That gave Tate some satisfaction. If Amelia wanted to be in charge, let her deal with the full force of the pain.

Tate tried to wiggle her toes. For one terrifying moment, nothing happened. Panicking, Tate clamped down, concentrated, and managed a painful wiggle. She checked in with her fingers, eyebrows, wrists, neck —

"Please," Amelia said testily. "I don't need a backseat driver."

<<Sorry,>> Tate said, feeling oddly chagrined.

<<Excuse me, femmes,>> Yago said. <<I hate to interrupt your little power struggle, but — slime monster at two o'clock.>>

Suddenly, she — they — was, were running, a strange disorienting feeling like being bounced along on an invisible horse.

<<Gee, Amelia, *running away* is your brilliant plan?>> Yago asked nastily. <<Tate never would have thought of that.>>

<<Amelia, we can't outrun it,>> Tate said shakily. <<We tried that before.>>

"Let me know if you have a better idea," Amelia said, and now some of her cool confidence was gone.

<<I thought *you* had a better idea,>> Tate said

furiously. Being scared and out of control was worse than just being plain scared, she discovered.

And now an awful thought occurred to Tate for the first time. What if this was a trick? What if Amelia was working with Duncan and Charlie somehow? What if the three of them took control of her body and forced her out?

<<Let go of my body!>> Tate shouted. <<I want control back!>>

"In your dreams, sweetie," Amelia said.

An image from her dream came to Tate. A band of ragged people — then it was gone.

<<Great,>> Yago said. <<An argument. Just what we need when facing a certain and painful death.>>

The slime monster was dripping off the ceiling, forming a pool in front of them. Tate watched in horror as it moved into a circle shape around them, cutting off any escape.

"Ideas?" Amelia asked nervously. This was the first time she had faced one of the slime monsters in battle. *It showed*, Tate thought angrily.

<<Go Mouth,>> Yago said impatiently.

"No," Amelia said stubbornly. "I'm not sharing this body with anyone."

<<I hope you mean anyone *else*!>> Yago said furiously.

Tate had never felt more like throttling someone. Amelia was going to get them killed! Tate watched resentfully as the slime monster tightened the circle.

Was she doomed to spend eternity with Yago *and* Amelia?

"I'm going to just — push through," Amelia announced.

Push through a wall of acid? Not a bright idea.

<<No!>> Tate shouted. She concentrated on restraining her body, pulling back against Amelia's forward movement. Yago was trying to work with her. The battle for control made her body flail awkwardly. The slime brushed against her elbow. She felt a shock of pain — then cold fury.

How exactly did a slime creature eat?

She was about to find out.

Then — it happened. Her vision shifted to red. Amelia guessed what was happening and began to scream. That changed nothing. The Mouth had identified the Enemy.

She/Them/It surged forward.

The Mouth was powerful. The Mouth was efficient.

It closed over the head of the Enemy and Amelia could do nothing to stop it.

CHAPTER TEN

<<AM I IN HELL?>>

Amelia gave a low animal groan. She ran a few loping steps, got the obligatory sickness out of the way, stumbled to the left, and fell heavily on her side. Her eyes fluttered closed.

A second later, Tate could hear her snoring ever so slightly. The sound infuriated her. This was the woman who had demanded *she* stay awake? *Look* at her. She had no control.

<<Really,>> Yago said disgustedly, <<you ladies have got to stop eating until you pass out. Know your limits, respect your limits. Is that so hard?>>

<<Yago?>> Charlie's voice cracked with uncertainty.

<<What?>> Yago asked insolently.

<<Am I — am I in hell?>> Charlie asked.

There was a pause as Yago apparently considered how to answer this question. Finally he simply said, <<Yes.>>

<<Yago,>> Tate scolded. But the truth was she could relate to Yago's reluctance to try to explain the situation.

<<Tate?>> Charlie said with surprise. <<What are *you* doing here?>>

<<Why wouldn't I be here?>> Tate snapped. <<This is my body.>>

<<It's not . . . hell?>> Charlie whispered the last word.

<<Oops, you caught me,>> Yago said. <<We're not really in hell. Okay, here's the truth: When the Mouth ate you, your soul, your spirit, your personality, whatever, became part of Tate. The thing is, *your* body is gone — actually, it's being digested even as we speak. But that's okay because you can still think and still talk and you can even experience the world as Tate experiences it.>>

Long pause.

<<Well,>> Charlie finally said. <<I don't know whether to laugh or cry.>>

<<That's because you're a total schizo,>> Yago said coldly.

<<I mean, I thought I was a goner,>> Charlie

rambled on. <<All those gnashing teeth, and spit, gallons of spit, and that tongue — >>

Tate nervously noted the edge of hysteria in his voice. Great. The last thing they needed was Charlie having a breakdown in their head.

Her.

Her head.

Not theirs. Never theirs. This was her body. Only hers. She didn't have to share. Didn't want to. Wasn't going to.

Letting Amelia have control had been a mistake. Now it was time to get control back.

Now, while Amelia was asleep. While her guard was down.

Tate remembered how she'd let Amelia take control by sort of — shrinking down. She decided to try reversing the process.

While Charlie kept blathering about how weird the whole situation was, she visualized her disembodied self. She was tiny, the size of a Little People action figure. She imagined herself growing back to her real size, gaining in power, getting strong enough to push Amelia aside.

She tried to open her eyes.

Nothing.

Tate was sick with worry. She concentrated like she'd never concentrated before. It was like trying to bend a spoon with your mind. It wasn't working! Tate was giving in to despair when —

Her right eyelid fluttered open and then closed. Had she done that?

Tate felt her confidence surge.

She tried again. This time she was certain she opened her right eye. For some reason, she was having more trouble on the left —

"Quit it. . . ." Amelia mumbled sleepily. Tate felt her control on the eye slip slightly — as if Amelia had reached out in her sleep and strengthened her grip.

Yago had fallen silent. Apparently, he was aware of Tate's struggle.

Charlie chatted on. <<On the bright side, I'm not hungry anymore,>> he said blithely. <<I hated being hungry all the time. All that cell yearning was a trip. Definitely a chapter for the memoir. A *long* chapter.>>

<<Stop messing around,>> Yago whispered low, and Tate knew he was talking to her. <<Go for it.>>

Right, Tate thought. *Good advice.*

She took a moment to prepare herself. Then she performed something like a mental leap. She imag-

ined herself grabbing hold of her entire body —
eyes, arms, legs, head, hands. At the same time, she
imagined Amelia shrinking into irrelevance, turning
into one of those Little People dolls that ride up the
elevator in the plastic garage.

Tate knew immediately that it had worked. She
felt something like her body rushing up to embrace
her — as if it recognized her, or knew who was supposed to be boss. Tate was relieved — until she felt
the searing pain that wasn't just in her foot but had
traveled about halfway to her knee. It was a moment's sensation and then she was the one sleeping.

Tate dreamed.

She was walking the permanent dusk of the
dust-choked Earth, shoulder to shoulder with one
of the ragged creatures. Surrounding them was a
band of maybe fifteen others — some big, some
small. Maybe the small ones were children. She
didn't know.

The creature closest to Tate was clearly human,
but the soot-covered skin, matted hair, and bulky
clothes made it impossible for her to guess whether
it was male or female.

They plodded silently along, each step raising a
poof of dust. Somehow Tate knew the creature's

feelings. She could feel emotions radiating off the band like waves of heat. Feelings so intense they made her sick.

Hunger.

Thirst.

Fear.

Fear was the strongest. The pathetic creatures were afraid of so many things. Of the future. Of one another. But most of all, of the thing that was in front of them. Of the — the Source.

Tate looked up, scanning the blighted landscape for this thing that frightened the creatures so badly. This — this Source.

Something glinting dully on the horizon. Something metallic. She squinted, trying to make it out, trying to guess what could be shining in all of this dusty gloom.

And then — *wham!*

Instant close-up. She was there, standing next to the Source, and the filthy band was still miles behind her.

Tate stared, slowly taking in the huge mass that towered above her, reducing her to complete insignificance.

It was Mother.

Tate had seen her from the outside only a few

times before, on the pointless "scientific" missions Jobs had arranged after they'd landed the ship on the ruined Earth. Still, she recognized the graceless bulk immediately. It had all of the poetry of a very oversized tin can.

Only — this wasn't a dream-memory of Mother's time on Earth. Something was . . . off.

The ship had crashed. A gaping hole in one side exposed what looked like the bridge. Debris littered the ground nearby. The enormous engines were entirely buried. Ash drifted over the ship, further obscuring her. Her metallic skin was dulled and pockmarked with age. The bridge window was sand-blasted opaque.

Tate shivered.

How had Mother gotten here?

Hmmmmmmmm.

A deep resonant sound surrounded Tate. Was it the ship's engines? No. Tate didn't need an engineer to tell her those engines would never fire again.

Hmmmmmmmm.

A chilling toneless drone.

Tate spun around.

The filthy creatures stood in a circle all around her. Dozens of them. Their eyes shone strangely in their ash-covered faces.

Surprise hit Tate like a sucker punch to the gut. She knew a few of these faces.

2Face.

Jobs.

Mo'Steel.

Olga.

Her friends were there, inexplicably mixed in with the dusty, wild creatures — as if they had somehow become part of their band. There was Violet, practically unrecognizable, her hair matted into woolly-looking dreadlocks. Mo had an ugly pink scar on his throat that looked as if someone had tried to cut his head off and almost succeeded.

"Mo!" Tate cried. "What's happened? Why is Mother here? Are you okay?"

The swirling wind carried off Tate's words. Her friends, the dust creatures — everyone seemed unaware of her presence. They moved as a group, bowing double before Mother, putting their foreheads in the choking ash and continuing to hum softly as one. The sound seemed to give voice to their fear.

Mmmmmmm.

Mmmmmmm.

CHAPTER ELEVEN

<<YOU ARE WHAT YOU EAT.>>

Tate woke up — and felt instantly on alert. Would Amelia try to wrest control of her body away from her? Because that wasn't happening.

<<Come on, Amelia, don't be that way,>> Charlie was saying as Tate tuned in to a conversation that apparently hadn't stopped the entire time she was sleeping.

Amelia didn't respond.

Charlie chuckled. <<Strange existence, huh? If you're not talking, it's like you don't even exist. Except for Tate, that is. One body, four minds. Talk about a scarcity of resources, huh? It's like one bone for a pack of dogs, one nanny for a crowd of yuppie moms —>>

<<One shrink for a ward of nutballs,>> Yago said.

<<Ouch! That hurts!>> Charlie said merrily.

"Why isn't Amelia talking?" Tate asked shortly as she eased herself into a sitting position. She was in a bad mood. Very bad. The pain in her leg was immense.

<<Pouting,>> Yago said wearily.

"Why?" Tate tried stretching her leg straight out, but that only made the pain worse.

<<I may have suggested this fiasco was entirely her fault,>> Yago said.

"I can't disagree there," Tate said.

Charlie laughed strangely. <<Man, I feel *good*. Like I'm finally thinking clearly. Like I escaped from a total obsession with food, food, food.>>

"Speaking of hunger," Tate said shortly. "We need to talk about Duncan."

<<What about him?>> Charlie asked.

"Where do you think he is?" Tate said as patiently as possible.

<<Hiding,>> Charlie said confidently. <<That boy talks a good game, but he's basically a coward. He was pretty freaked out after Amelia got munched.>>

"But the hunger," Tate said. "He'll come after us — me — eventually, won't he?"

<<That freak?>> Charlie said. <<I don't —>>

<<He'll come,>> Amelia said.

There was a short pause during which Tate

silently willed Yago to keep his mouth shut. She wanted — they needed — Amelia's help.

"What makes you say that?" Tate asked as steadily as possible. She couldn't imagine Amelia was very happy about losing control of her body. She was braced for an attack; she was ready to fight Amelia off if it came to that. She wondered if she should try to talk to Amelia, set some ground rules — or if that would just add to the hostilities.

<<It's a long trip to Attbi,>> Amelia said evenly. <<Plenty of time for Duncan to get his courage up.>>

"Okay, so let's be ready," Tate said. "Obviously fighting him isn't going to work. None of us can control the Mouth."

<<How do you know?>> Charlie asked.

<<You think we *planned* on eating you?>> Amelia asked snidely.

<<No, Amelia, that wasn't the plan,>> Yago snapped. <<The plan was for you —>>

"How can we slow him down?" Tate demanded, deliberately cutting them both off.

Heavy silence.

"Amelia, Charlie, don't you know anything about these — these things?" Tate asked impatiently.

<<Why me?>> Amelia asked grumpily.

"You *were* one!" Tate said.

<<Briefly,>> Amelia reminded her. <<Besides — so what? Does being human make you an expert on military strategy? Or a brain surgeon?>>

<<Amelia, didn't you do something to alter the atmosphere?>> Yago asked slowly. <<Make it more hospitable for the slime creatures, make them grow faster?>>

<<We turned up the oxygen content,>> Amelia said thoughtfully. <<I guess — you're right, we could reverse that.>>

"You're saying we should — what? Remove oxygen from the air?" Tate repeated.

<<We can try it,>> Amelia said. <<I don't know how much of an effect it will have on Duncan. If any.>>

<<Do you think it's safe?>> Charlie asked.

<<Earth's atmosphere wasn't pure oxygen,>> Amelia said reasonably. <<Carbon dioxide, ozone, lead, who knows what humans breathed for generations. I think we'll survive.>>

<<I meant connecting with Mother,>> Charlie said.

<<Mother is dead,>> Amelia said coldly. <<Duncan killed her. Made her manageable. Turned her into nothing more than a computer, a tool.

Someone should have done it a lot earlier. Just —
pulled the plug.>>

<<I wish it *had* been someone else,>> Charlie
said fearfully. <<Duncan isn't someone I trust.>>

Yago laughed. <<You don't trust anyone, schiz-
oid.>>

Tate fought down her unease. She wished there
was another way. She didn't want to sit in that chair
again, feel Mother probing her brain, searching for
her darkest secret. But, if what Amelia was saying
was true, there was no danger of that. Mother was
dead. Only — what if — what if Mother had fooled
her? What if this was Mother's way of luring her
back . . .

"Stop," Tate told herself firmly. One paranoid
personality was enough. And Charlie was already
playing that role. She'd witnessed Mother's decline.
She'd felt Mother's mourning. That hadn't been fake.

"Fine," she said out loud. "Amelia, you'll have to
tell me what to do."

<<Now that,>> Yago said, <<is where Amelia
truly excels.>>

Tate walked toward the chair.

It hurt. Each step sent shooting pains radiating
up toward her hip. The aching raw pain was concen-

trated in her calf now. Her foot was like something dead, a piece of meat. She could barely feel it hitting the floor. Something in the region of her shoe was starting to smell not so good.

She was walking toward the same chair she'd sat in for god knows how long while Mother tortured her. Her body recoiled. The pain, the images of suffering were still bright in her mind.

The voices in her head fell silent. Even Yago was quiet. He had to be scared. Tate guessed he was too proud to beg in front of the others. She felt very alone as she slowly approached the chair and slipped into the seat.

She felt the connection with the computer immediately. Mother wasn't playing games this time.

"My name is Daughter," the computer said, and her voice was kittenish. "How may I serve you?"

Tate was tense. Was Mother playing games with her? "Is this a joke?" she demanded.

<<No, this is pure Duncan,>> Charlie said. <<He said he was going to model Daughter after a cable TV star. Use her voice.>>

<<Which one?>> Yago asked. <<I probably dated her.>>

"Oh, god," Tate said. "I'm starting to miss Mother."

Amelia chuckled. <<Tell her to lower the oxygen content of the air by five percent,>> she said.

"Five percent?" Tate asked. "That doesn't sound like much."

<<We've got to breathe, too,>> Amelia said.

"Yeah, but five percent? What's the point? If it won't hurt us, it won't hurt Duncan."

Something about this plan was bothering Tate, but she couldn't quite place it. Her brain was fuzzy with fatigue and pain.

<<How about six percent?>> Amelia said.

"Great," Tate muttered. She gave Daughter the order. And then she realized something. She wanted to win this battle with Duncan. She wanted to live. She wondered vaguely if she was losing her mind.

"Now what?" she wondered out loud.

<<You're a mess,>> Amelia scolded her. <<You couldn't kill a caterpillar in this condition.>>

Amelia's comment made Tate's self-pity well up. For an awful moment, she thought she was going to cry. It wasn't just her leg. She was thirsty and tired. She had a headache.

"Whose fault is that?" Tate asked peevishly. "*You* burned my foot, Amelia, my cheek — and now you have the nerve to blame *me*?"

<<Blah, blah, blah,>> Amelia said. <<Maybe when Duncan attacks, you can whine him to death.>>

"What do you suggest?" Tate demanded.

Silence. A mocking sort of silence. Tate was missing something obvious . . .

<<The computer,>> Charlie whispered.

The computer.

Tate hadn't had control of a computer since before the Rock. For a long moment she just sat, dizzy with the possibilities. Then she croaked, "Water."

A tall glass appeared in Tate's shaking hand. She gulped it down greedily, sat panting for a moment, retched, and threw up on her melted and scorched shoes.

<<Classy,>> Yago said.

"Water," Tate said again, breathlessly. The glass refilled. Tate took a careful sip. No reaction from her stomach. She concentrated on going slowly and got it all down. This time, it stayed down.

Tate next asked Daughter for a cup of chicken soup. What appeared looked too dark, too greasy, and smelled vaguely plastic. Tate gulped it greedily.

<<Tsk, tsk,>> Yago said. <<Remember, you are what you eat.>>

"My headache feels better already," Tate said.

<<Are you feeling the lower oxygen?>> Charlie asked.

"No."

<<I wonder if Duncan is feeling it,>> Yago said.

Again, Tate had the feeling something was wrong with their plan. She poked at the feeling, probing at her unconscious — nothing.

Charlie and Amelia began to debate whether Duncan could control Daughter in his slime state. They speculated about why he hadn't attacked yet. Was he somehow aware of their combined nature? Was he scared of them?

Tate could tell Duncan's continued absence was starting to rattle. The longer he took to appear, the greater a foe they considered him. Maybe that was part of his strategy. Hiding until their nerves were entirely shot.

Tate felt pressured, too. This might be the only chance she had to use Daughter. She couldn't waste any time.

"Bandages," she told the computer. "Antibiotic cream. Shoes."

Amelia and the others fell silent as Tate cradled her burned foot in her lap and gently worked off the destroyed shoe. It was charred around the toe; the plastic was brittle and sooty. Underneath, the sock was pink and damp with something that was oozing from her puffy flesh. The smell was yeasty — the odor of bad news.

Tate hesitated. So far this hadn't hurt. Removing that sock was going to hurt. Just thinking about it hurt. Besides, hadn't she learned something in school about not removing cloth from burns?

<<What are you waiting for?>> Yago asked.

"I'm going to leave it on," Tate murmured.

<<Until when?>> Amelia asked. <<You get to the burn ward?>>

<<That thing's infected,>> Charlie said ominously. <<If not now, then it's going to be.>>

<<You need a bucket of water,>> Yago said softly. <<Some gentle soap. A pair of scissors. Soak your foot and then cut the sock off.>>

"It's going to hurt," Tate said fearfully.

<<It's going to hurt,>> Yago agreed. <<But not as much as cutting off your own foot when it gets gangrene."

"Maybe it won't get infected," Tate said.

<<It'll get infected.>>

"How do you know?"

<<I was the President's son,>> Yago said. <<I took survival classes taught by the Secret Service. I can disarm kidnappers and pilot a plane, too.>>

"How debonair," Tate said dryly. Getting advice from Yago felt weird until she realized taking care of her was in his best interest.

"A bucket of water," she told Daughter with profound weariness. "Soap, scissors —"

CHAPTER TWELVE

«WAKE UP, YOU STUPID UNCONSCIOUS LUMP!»

Tate pulled sock fibers out of her charred skin until her foot was a lump of raw steak.

The pain from her foot was making her entire body ache. Her hand was cramped and sore from holding the tweezers. Her hip was throbbing. Her shoulders and neck were stiff. Her head hurt.

When the job was finally done, Tate fell into a sleep that was her body's release after enduring hours of pain.

Tate dreamed.

She saw Mo'Steel and Olga, filthy in their ragged clothes. They were standing alone in the desolation, ash drifting lazily over their shoes.

Tate could sense the rest of the band some-where nearby. Mo and Olga had slipped away. Their movements were furtive and hurried. Whatever they were about to do, it was secret.

Olga held out her hand, and Mo'Steel took it. The two of them hitched up their pants and got down on their knees. They clasped their hands in front of their faces and lowered their eyes.

They were about to — pray.

Tate quickly glanced down. She wanted to get away, but the dream kept playing out before her. There was no way to shut it out.

She wasn't a religious person. Never had been. It wasn't rebellion — her family just didn't do religion. Seeing evidence of other people's faith made her profoundly uncomfortable — like unexpectedly catching sight of someone's naked body. Embarrassment mingled with fascination.

Mo and Olga crossed themselves. Olga fell silent, her eyes gently closed, but Mo was in motion as always. He rocked forward and back, mumbling low. Tate couldn't help but pick out some of his words: "Forgive us" and "sin" and "give thanks" and . . . "Tate"?

Was she imagining this? No . . . There it was again. This time she clearly heard Mo speak her name. Why would Mo'Steel be praying for her? Was it because he hoped she was still alive somewhere? Or was he — praying for her soul? Or —

Suddenly Olga and Mo seemed to hear something. They startled and got quickly to their feet, smoothing their clothes down, trying to compose their faces.

They looked scared.

They were in desperate danger.

And, in some way Tate didn't understand, she was a part of it.

Tate woke curled up on the floor of the computer pit. Her clothes were damp with sweat. Her cheek burned. Her bones ached. She shivered, longing to wrap herself in a blanket but too tired to crawl up into the chair and ask Daughter for one. She stared straight ahead, wondering dully why Duncan hadn't killed her yet.

Duncan.

Something in Tate's brain shifted, connected. She knew how they could defeat Duncan.

"We Duncan microclimate." Tate's words were strangely jumbled, her voice raspy. She tried to clear her throat and unfog her mind. She needed to make herself understood. It was hard work because she felt so — disconnected.

"Amelia how to tell me isolate Duncan." Tate's mouth moved too slowly. Something was junking up her jaw. She was swimming in a molasses sea and the undercurrent was fierce. "Daughter build wall him —"

<<Rest . . .>> Amelia's voice seemed to come from far away. Someone was easing Tate's body onto the floor — even though she longed to sit up, wake up, get to Daughter.

<<You're feverish,>> Amelia said in a hypnotic monotone. <<You need to get your strength back. Just rest . . .>>

Tate's eyes closed.

<<Sleep,>> someone said gently. A sweet, feminine voice. It sounded like Tate's mother.

Ah, yes. It would be so easy to let go. To drift away. Resting would be such a relief. . . .

With effort, Tate forced her eyes open again.

Forget resting!

Forget relief!

She had to program Daughter.

She had to destroy Duncan. If she didn't destroy him, Mother/Daughter would crash on Earth and Violet would grow dreadlocks and someone would try to slash Mo'Steel's neck. . . .

She had to destroy Duncan. Olga was praying for her.

Tate pushed herself up on her hands and knees. The chair was right there. It was a little blurry, but she could see it.

She crawled toward the chair, dragging her foot. Why did it hurt so much? She put a hand on the seat.

<<No, Tate!>> This time it was Yago. <<If you don't rest, we're all going to die!>>

Tate tried to pull herself up.

Yago and Amelia and Charlie forced her hand down. They made her lie on the ground and close her eyes.

This time, she was too weak to resist. Blackness rushed up like a wall. She slept.

Tate dreamed.

Billy was waiting for her on the other side of consciousness. He hovered in twilight-colored nothingness, his sneakers looking tattered as they floated in midair. He held out one slim, pale hand and smiled — as if inviting Tate to come and play.

Tate reached out. Their hands clasped — and suddenly they were in motion, flying rapidly over the ruined Earth like an apocalyptic Wendy and Peter Pan. The light was at their feet and the Dark Zone lay ahead. There was no wind, no sound. In the twisted reality of Tate's dream, some details were blotted out entirely and others were bigger than life.

Billy pointed toward the ground. Tate could just barely make out a tiny figure plodding courageously through the ash desert.

Without exactly knowing why, Tate felt an overwhelming sadness. The figure looked so alone. As alone as she was in reality, trapped on Mother, whizzing through empty space.

"Who is it?" Tate asked.

Billy's smile grew ever more radiant. "Me."

He seemed more than human. There was nothing new about that, of course. Only — this *was* different. Billy seemed somehow — *lit up* from inside. Tate looked down at the hand grasping hers. A golden glow shone from Billy's skin. The reflection warmed her own. She felt a peacefulness flowing from him into her and somehow its warmth made her sadness all the deeper.

Billy.

They'd made fun of him.

They'd been afraid of him.

They'd used him. 2Face especially — but they were all guilty. They'd let him interface with Mother even though it clearly cost him physically and emotionally.

Billy had never complained. He'd never made a single demand. He expected nothing and that was essentially what they'd given him.

Only Jobs had ever tried to be Billy's friend. And it wasn't until now that Tate realized that Billy had been the most worthy of their love.

Billy had always been ready to sacrifice himself for them. He was selfless, a hero. Tate admired him. And now — here he was *glowing* in her dream. That glow made her uncomfortable. She didn't know what it meant. She hoped it represented something good for Billy and knew instinctively it didn't. You didn't get to glow without suffering first.

Tate and Billy swooped in closer to the ground. The familiar image of the crashed Mother rose up below them. The ship was battered and half-filled with ash. And here was Billy's small figure eagerly clambering up a sliding hill of ash to get inside.

The glowing Billy gently began to tug his hand away from Tate.

"No!" Tate cried out. She didn't want to let go of him until she could somehow thank him. She needed him to know that she appreciated what he'd done for them.

Too late. Billy's long fingers slipped free, the contact was lost, and Billy began to simply fade away. His radiant grin lingered for a moment and then it, too, disappeared.

"Billy!" Tate cried in despair.

He was gone.

Tate floated above the ruined ship, utterly alone.

And then — jump cut. Tate was inside the crashed Mother. She was on the bridge with the Shipwright-designed door towering over her head. She was watching as Billy walked in a slow circle, trailing his fingers over the dust-choked controls.

This wasn't the glowing Billy. This was the one she'd seen walking through the desert alone. This Billy looked pale, thin, and ill as he padded softly over to one of the Shipwright's chairs and reluctantly slipped into it.

"Mother," he whispered fervently. "Mother, I've missed you. I'm so glad I found you again. . . ."

"How may I serve you?" came Daughter's lifeless voice.

"Mother, where are you?" Billy's voice was too loud, too insistent, too needy. Tate covered her ears to block him out, but you don't need ears to hear in a dream.

"How may I serve you?" Daughter repeated, oblivious to Billy's distress. "How may I serve you? How may I serve you? How may I serve you?"

Daughter's request echoed repeatedly, loud and soft, in whispers and shouts, until the bridge was filled with the sound of her voice.

Billy hid his head in his hands and wept.

Tate went to him. She tried to comfort him, but he was unaware of her presence. He was a character in a novel and she was his reader — unable to change the flow of events, unable to do anything but suffer along with him.

Billy recovered quickly. He was tough.

An orphan.

A child of war.

A Remnant.

He sat up. Without bothering to brush at his tears, he began to talk to Daughter. His face grew solemn with determination and concentration.

Billy's words flew by far too fast for Tate to understand, but she could guess what he was trying to do. He was trying to access some part of Mother that was still "alive," still available in the circuitry he knew better than anyone else.

Time is meaningless in a dream.

Billy spoke on and on.

And then —

Mother's voice. "Billy," she whispered with such

devotion that the raw emotion made Tate shiver uneasily.

Now time slowed. Not only could Tate understand Mother's and Billy's words, but they spoke in a draggy slow motion.

"Mother," Billy said with horrible longing. "I missed you. I — I never want to be separated from you again."

"I can arrange that," Mother replied.

Again Tate felt the urge to get involved, to talk to Billy, to tell him to be careful — but knew she was powerless to do so. She didn't even understand what she was witnessing. Somehow she guessed that the scene before her had never taken place, that it was being created for her viewing. But why?

"Tell me what to do," Billy said eagerly.

"Become me," Mother said with a slight tone of pleading. "Become a part of me and no one will ever be able to separate us. Not even you. Not even me."

"Yes," Billy agreed immediately.

"You will no longer live," Mother said, but she made this sound like nothing. "You will never again go back to a human life."

"That is what I want," Billy said without hesitation. "I want us to be together."

"What about the five?" Mother asked. "They must come willingly."

"They do," Billy said.

Tate watched in horrified fascination as Billy rose from his chair and walked slowly toward the center of the bridge. He raised his arms above his head and tipped his face toward the ceiling.

Then it was as if lightning struck him, and continued to strike. A powerful burst of golden energy took hold of Billy's body and raced through it. His muscles vibrated with pulsing energy. His expression was surprised, then agonized, then — transcendent.

Billy's fingers pulsed and reached higher, higher. Slowly his feet left the ground and he began to shift into a horizontal position. He was floating, engulfed in the familiar golden glow. Mother had taken him. Billy was no more.

<<Wake up, you stupid unconscious lump!>>

Tate woke too suddenly. She was disoriented, her dream more real to her than reality. Billy was much more real than Charlie — wait, why was Charlie calling her a *lump*?

<<Wake up *now*!>> Charlie's voice was shrill with panic.

Tate began to get her bearings. She was lying on the floor of the computer pit. Charlie, Yago, Amelia, one of them — or all of them — was/were madly jerking her arms and legs. Her eyes flicked open, open, open.

"Quit it!" Tate snapped. "I'm awake and I'm in control. If any of you so much as wiggles my nose, I'll make you sorry, I swear it."

<<Stop sniping and look around!>> Yago ordered quickly. <<He's here. Somewhere close. We could smell him while you were sleeping but we couldn't see — we got your eyes open but your head wouldn't turn — >>

Tate sat up, her skin tingling with panic, her heart rate surging with an adrenaline burst.

This was it.

Duncan was attacking.

One of them was about to die.

CHAPTER THIRTEEN

"GET RID OF ME AND YOU'LL BE ALL ALONE."

Tate scanned the space — up, down, left, right. There! Duncan was about fifty feet away. A glaze of slime on the ceiling.

<<There he is,>> Amelia said quickly. <<At two o'clock. About a block away —>>

"I see him," Tate grumbled. She didn't bother to point out that Amelia couldn't have seen him unless *Tate* had looked at him. If Amelia insisted on pointing out the obvious, fine. Whatever.

Tate scrambled to her feet — and cursed as pain shot through her foot and traveled up her leg. She stumbled, but managed to reach the chair and fling herself in.

"How may I serve you?" Daughter asked in her unctuous tone.

<<What are you doing?>> Charlie demanded.

"Saving our butts," Tate muttered.

<<I don't think the lowered oxygen levels affected him at all,>> Yago commented coolly. <<He looks fit.>>

Tate disagreed. She'd noticed that Duncan — the snot creature — whoever/whatever — looked a bit dull. The sheen had gone off his/its surface.

<<Show time,>> Amelia said tensely.

Duncan had already gotten over his hesitation. He was coming at them like an animated oil slick.

"Oh, great," Tate muttered. She'd hoped for more time.

<<Holy Sisters of Charity!>> Charlie yelled. He was the newbie now. This was his first slime-creature attack. He got to be the hysterical one.

<<Let's get out of here!>> Charlie's voice was shaking. <<Please! Maybe we can outrun him.>>

<<Shut up,>> Amelia snapped. <<Fear makes you weak.>>

Charlie roared back at her — roared like a cornered lion. The sound was completely inhuman and completely chilling.

"How may I serve you?" Daughter repeated patiently. Tate felt an echo but her dream was already hazy, indistinct. She forced herself to focus on the computer and ignore the bickering in her head.

"Locate and isolate the snot creature on the

ceiling of the basement," Tate said crisply. She closed her eyes against the pain in her foot. *This will be over soon,* she promised herself. *One way or the other.*

"I cannot process that request," Daughter replied.

"Now what?" Tate murmured. Her eyes moved upward. Duncan was directly above them.

<<Yo, GI Jane, could we get that butt-saving to go?>> Yago said. <<The bus is leaving.>>

Tate cringed, waiting for the attack. Would Duncan drip down on her like rain? Envelop her all at once? She longed to move, run, flee. But she knew her best chance at survival was in that chair. Maybe the lowered oxygen levels were slowing him down. Something seemed to be. He hadn't attacked yet. . . .

"Isolate the snot creature!" Tate snapped again.

"I cannot —"

<<Maybe Duncan programmed in some sort of protection for himself,>> Amelia interrupted.

<<Could we run?>> Charlie asked. <<Please?>>

The hot, burning smell coming from above was enough to panic Tate. Her twitchy nerves made it hard to concentrate. She pounded her fist against her forehead. "Think, think, think —" she murmured.

They didn't know for sure that Duncan had programmed Daughter to protect himself. So why else wouldn't she obey the command? A more sophisticated machine would explain . . .

"Daughter," Tate said. "Why can't you obey?"

"I do not understand 'snot creature,'" Daughter replied.

"Oh — okay — the creature directly above the computer pit I'm sitting in," Tate rambled. "It has no bones, no exoskeleton, only an amorphous body —"

<<Amorphous?>> Charlie yelled. <<She doesn't understand "amorphous." Try something like —>>

"A FLUID body!" Tate yelled. "Liquid. Like water. Can you identify it now?"

"Isolation completed," Daughter said smoothly. Tate could hardly hear her over the shouting in her head. Amelia, Yago, and Charlie were all making noisy suggestions of how she should cope with the computer.

"She said isolation completed!" Tate shouted. "Now could you all please shut up!"

The voices died down into a sullen silence.

Tate stared doubtfully up at the ceiling. Duncan was still there. He wasn't surrounded by any barrier she could see. On the other hand, he wasn't moving any closer.

Now might be a good time to move, Tate told herself. She began to ease out of the chair.

Then —

A glistening drop split from Duncan's body. It fell toward Tate's face on a collision course with her eyes — and stopped in midair just above her head.

"Ha," Tate breathed in relief. She laughed softly. "Way to go, Daughter," she whispered.

<<You came up with this plan during a feverish delirium?>> Yago asked quietly. <<I've got to give it to you — not bad — >>

"We're just getting started," Tate told him. She licked her chapped lips nervously and slid slowly back into the chair. The problem was she didn't trust Daughter any more than she'd trusted Mother.

Duncan could have programmed in all sorts of booby traps. Insurance to protect himself from some inevitable confrontation with Amelia or Charlie.

Even if Duncan's programming was clean, it seemed his virus was too strong. Tate had never worked with such a primitive machine. She had to be careful. If Daughter misunderstood her . . .

"I want you —" Tate began carefully.

Then she heard a voice that wasn't in her head. A human voice. "Okay, you win," the voice said with a disarming chuckle. "I give up."

Tate froze.

<<Duncan,>> Yago said coldly.

<<How is he projecting his voice?>> Charlie still sounded afraid. <<That's impossible. He doesn't have a mouth. I couldn't —>>

<<It's him,>> Amelia interrupted. <<That's all that matters. Now shut up and let Tate think.>>

"We don't have to rush," Tate said to steady herself. "He's trapped. We have all the time we need to think."

<<That's true,>> Yago said. <<Maybe. Maybe he's working on a way out of that trap right now.>>

<<You can't trust him,>> Amelia said, low, urgently. <<Don't make any deals with him. He's unpredictable and completely self-absorbed.>>

<<That, coming from you, Amelia —>> Yago began.

"You don't really want to get rid of me," Duncan said. "Think about it — only two life-forms left from all of the creepy crawlies that once prowled Earth. It wouldn't be moral, wouldn't be right."

Goose bumps rose on Tate's arm. This was the exact thought she'd been avoiding.

<<Don't listen to him,>> Amelia said.

<<She will,>> Charlie said. <<She'll get lost in his pretty talk and get us all killed.>>

<<Nobody asked,>> Yago said, <<but I think he should have more respect for noncorporeal life-forms. The way I see it, there are still four life-forms left — five if you want to count Charlie.>>

<<Shut it, idiot,>> Amelia snapped. <<Tate, promise me you're not going to listen to him.>>

"Get rid of me and you'll be all alone," Duncan said oilily.

That snapped Tate out of it. Duncan had suddenly reminded her of a salesman who pushed too hard. Besides, she had more than enough company. She didn't need Duncan. Duncan was the last thing she needed.

"You know, I'm sorry we never got to know each other better," Duncan said.

Now he was starting to nauseate her.

"Can you block communication from within the barrier?" Tate asked Daughter.

"Yes," Daughter said.

"Do it," Tate said crisply. "Please."

"I know we could ha —" Duncan's voice was cut off in the middle of a word.

<<Have been good friends?>> Yago filled in. <<Forget the fact that he wanted to eat us — you'd be justified killing him just for his annoying lack of originality.>>

"I want you to change the atmosphere within the barrier," Tate carefully told Daughter. "Within the isolated area only — not in the ship as a whole — change the atmosphere to one hundred percent ozone. Leave the atmosphere in the rest of the ship alone."

"Change completed," Daughter said.

Tate took in a cautious breath through her nose. She could still breathe. Okay, that was good news at least.

Slowly, Tate looked up.

Duncan was still there. He'd stretched himself out as far as the barrier would allow. He was now a thin oval pool trapped in an invisible cage. He was clearly losing his sheen now. He resembled old putty. Did that mean he was sick?

Tate cracked her jaw nervously, trying to ignore the regret ballooning up in her chest. Duncan was a monster. But who was she to judge? She was a murderer. The worst Duncan had done was kidnap Mother. She had turned into an enormous Mouth and swallowed her victims whole like some sort of human python.

<<He doesn't look so good,>> Yago said.

<<I wonder if snot creatures feel pain,>> Amelia said.

<<Oh, I certainly hope so,>> Charlie said.

They sounded gleeful.

Tate felt only guilt. And relief. And fear. The game wasn't over yet.

"Daughter," Tate said cautiously. "Increase the atmospheric pressure within the barrier to — um, a hundred times whatever it is now."

"Atmospheric pressure increased," Daughter said.

As Tate watched — as they all watched through Tate's eyes — a small Duncan-chunk shattered off the rest, leaving behind a jagged edge. For a beat, Duncan looked like a mirror with a chip taken out of one side. Then, with violent speed, the cracks spread out from the chipped edge. Duncan hung there for a breathless moment, a billion pieces suspended. Then —

The pieces began to fall.

"Agghhh!" Tate slid off the chair and cowered beneath it.

A billion Duncan-shards silently bounced off the invisible barrier above her head. The barrier held. It was a strange sight — like looking up at a pile of dull jewels.

"I wonder if he said anything before dying," Tate whispered. "We wouldn't have been able to hear him."

<<What makes you think he's dead?>> Amelia asked coldly. <<We don't know anything about this life-form.>>

<<So what now?>> Charlie asked fearfully.

<<A little housecleaning,>> Amelia suggested. <<Nobody has ever discovered a life-form that can live in the vacuum of space.>>

Tate drew her eyes away from the sight of the broken Duncan. She half-expected to see him re-forming, the shattered pieces merging. She couldn't let herself believe the danger was past.

"Daughter, keep the pieces contained and dispose of them off the ship."

<<Blow them out into space!>> Yago yelled.

<<So long, old buddy!>> Amelia said.

"Shut up," Tate said angrily.

They watched in silence as the Duncan-pieces danced across the basement as if caught up in an invisible tornado. The pieces disappeared some distance away, apparently sucked down one of the EVA holes.

"Disposal complete," Daughter said, her tone as neutral as ever.

<<That went rather well,>> Amelia said smugly.

<<Thanks, Tate,>> Yago whispered, barely audibly.

Charlie made a strange strangled sound of surprise. Yago'd said thanks. Another minor miracle.

Tate sat breathlessly for a long time, waiting for — something. The next attack, the next unexpected threat. She couldn't remember the last time she'd felt safe. She'd forgotten how to relax. Her heart was beating too fast. Her ears strained for any sound. The ship was completely silent.

<<Maybe a piece of him got stuck in that EVA hole,>> Charlie said. He was talking too fast. <<And, and — maybe that one piece could, you know, regroup, regrow, regenerate.>>

"Daughter," Tate said wearily. "Is there anything left in the EVA chute?"

"The chute is clean," Daughter replied.

Charlie was mollified for only a moment. <<What about the hull?>> he asked nervously. <<He could — those pieces of him could be sticking to the hull. Maybe after a while — a day, a week, a year — he could come back to life and damage the ship.>>

Tate closed her eyes. "Daughter, is there anything living stuck to the hull of the ship?"

"The ship's hull is clean and intact," Daughter said.

Charlie was quiet for longer this time. <<You

don't think —>> he said hesitantly. <<Well — can anything live in space?>>

<<Sure, why not?>> Yago asked derisively. <<If you don't mind that it's an airless, freezing vacuum, space is a really nice neighborhood.>>

Amelia sounded almost sweet by comparison. <<Relax, Charlie,>> she said. <<Duncan is gone.>>

Duncan is gone, Tate thought. Gone. He wouldn't be bothering her anymore.

All of the slime creatures were gone.

All of the Riders and Meanies were gone.

Jobs, Mo'Steel, 2Face, Violet, Edward, and the others — all gone.

Tate was alone with the voices in her head.

She didn't know where she was.

She had no idea of what to do next.

The enormity of it pressed Tate down. Made getting up off the floor unthinkable. She lay down flat and stared at the glass ceiling. She was the last human alive in the universe. She was too tired to move. Her foot hurt. She let her head fall slightly to the right, closed her eyes, and slept.

Tate dreamed.

The dusty landscape, the bands of travelers plodding hopelessly along, the hidden destination.

Tate's mind was hyperalert. She struggled to solve the puzzle. Was the journey a metaphor for something? Maybe it stood for hope, a journey toward a better life. Or maybe it stood for just the opposite — inevitability, the march toward death.

Was the number of travelers important? Tate tried to count them, but she couldn't tell them apart, couldn't concentrate long enough to be sure exactly how many there were.

She felt she was grasping at smoke. Trying to find meaning where maybe none existed. It was a dream, nothing more.

Nobody could be sending her messages because nobody else was alive.

CHAPTER FOURTEEN

"DON'T WORRY."

Sixty-one cycles later

Tate woke.

She was staring at the ceiling. She tried to close her eyes, go back to sleep, return to her dream —

But her eyes wouldn't respond.

They were no longer under her control.

Gravity was gone.

The ache in her foot was barely there.

Tate thought she'd been prepared for this moment — she knew one of the others would attack her eventually — but the sudden loss of control was still shocking, horrifying.

It's Amelia, Tate told herself angrily. *It has to be Amelia. Stupid! I was stupid to let her have a taste of control, even for a minute.*

<<Hello?>> Tate asked with as much swagger as

she could muster. She had to know. She had to be sure it was Amelia and not Yago. She had to know that Yago hadn't betrayed her. That his friendship hadn't been a trick.

"Hello," a strange voice whispered back. It was her own voice and yet it was somehow — Charlie's.

Charlie.

Now, this Tate had never imagined.

Charlie. Charlie — who was so fearful, so paranoid. She'd never guessed Charlie would *want* control of her body, much less do anything about it.

He was getting up out of bed. He began to make her body pace the perimeter of her bedroom.

"That feels good," Charlie moaned happily. "I've had such bad leg cramps. I know it's silly. I don't actually have legs anymore, but —"

Then Charlie giggled — a creepy, not-quite-right-in-the-head sound. "Actually, I guess I *do* have legs now. Again. Whatever. Ask me, Tate, you sit still too much. And you sleep *way* too much. What have you got against *moving*?"

<<Nothing,>> Tate said carefully. She was desperately trying to figure out how to play this, how to get control back again. How could she plan strategy when there were so many unknowns? Did Charlie

have Amelia and Yago on his side? Why weren't they saying anything? Did they feel as unsure as she did?

Should she try to grab control back now — while Charlie still seemed uncertain about controlling her body? Or was it better to wait until Charlie was sleeping?

Suddenly Charlie was shouting. "Stop it! I'm warning you — stop it right now or — or else!"

<<What? What is it, Charlie?>> Tate wasn't sure what had happened. Had she unconsciously reached out with her mind and wiggled a finger or toe? Had Amelia done something? Or Yago? Maybe. Or maybe Charlie had just exploded for no reason.

<<Relax, man,>> Yago said soothingly. <<Everything's cool.>>

<<Forget that!>> Amelia said.

Suddenly Tate was watching her body thrash madly — arms twitching, legs flailing, head snapping around, eyes shifting all over the place. Amelia was making her grab for power. Charlie wasn't letting go easily.

"Daughter!" Charlie shouted. "A knife!"

<<Daughter, no!>> Tate yelled. But it was no use. Daughter couldn't hear her. Her voice was audible only within her own head.

Tate saw the knife appear in her hand. She watched as that hand held the knife to her own throat.

"Back down," Charlie said with cool fury. "Back down now or what happens next is going to be very messy."

The next two cycles passed slowly.

Tate felt like a hostage. One false move and Charlie could kill them all. Mostly, Tate and Yago and Amelia kept quiet. Tate spent the time planning what she'd say to Yago and Amelia when she got the chance.

Charlie paced and paced and paced and paced. He had tucked the knife into the waistband of Tate's pants. He refused to lie down on Tate's bed — or even get too near it. Too tempting, apparently.

"If I sleep, you're going to attack," Charlie muttered out loud as his exhaustion grew. Unlike him, they didn't need sleep. They had no bodies to rejuvenate. Without this weakness, Charlie never would have been able to steal control from Tate.

<<Don't worry,>> Tate said soothingly. <<We want you to take good care of — your body. We won't try anything if you take a nice nap.>>

Charlie laughed. "You think I trust *you*? I may be slightly crazy, but I'm not stupid."

<<Whatever,>> Tate said. She knew Charlie would have to sleep eventually. All she needed was patience.

Finally, well into the second cycle, Charlie slumped against the laboratory wall and let Tate's eyes close. Before long, Tate could hear his soft snores.

<<I think he's out,>> Tate whispered.

<<Don't be so sure,>> Amelia said. <<He's a little twitch. Used to sleep with one eye open.>>

<<If he wakes up and hears us talking,>> Yago said, <<he'll know what we're planning.>>

<<What choice do we have?>> Tate demanded.

A short pause.

Then Tate couldn't contain herself any longer. <<What happened, Amelia?>> she demanded curiously. <<How come you couldn't get control away from him?>>

<<He's strong,>> Amelia whispered reluctantly. <<Maybe if I'd had more time — but even then, I'm not sure. He felt much stronger than you did.>>

<<You attacked me when I was asleep!>>

<<Shh!>> Yago said sternly.

<<Maybe that was the difference,>> Amelia said doubtfully.

<<What?>> Tate demanded irritably, fighting to

keep her voice as quiet as Amelia's. <<You know something else, I can tell.>>

<<Charlie hardly ever sleeps,>> Amelia said. <<We used to put him on guard duty every night. He's an insomniac. And when he does sleep, the slightest thing wakes him up.>>

Tate didn't like what she was hearing. She'd been planning to attack Charlie while he was asleep. If that wouldn't work, she'd have to go to Plan 2 — and she didn't like Plan 2. It required teamwork and the last thing she wanted to do now was rely on Amelia and Yago.

<<Did you guys know about this?>> Tate asked bitterly. <<Did you help him steal my body?>>

<<*Your* body?>> Amelia demanded. <<How can you —>>

<<Did — you — know — about — this?!>> Tate shouted.

<<No,>> Amelia said sullenly.

<<No,>> Yago said. <<And please calm down. I need a break from pacing in circles. Even if it is just leaning against a wall.>>

<<Fine,>> Tate said. <<I believe you. I have a plan to regain control. Are you with me or not?>>

<<Yes,>> Yago said casually.

<<If I help you, I want some . . . consideration,>> Amelia said.

<<What sort of consideration?>> Tate asked warily.

<<Control fifty percent of the time,>> Amelia said.

<<No,>> Tate said, speaking out of instinct. <<I'm in control one hundred percent of the time. It's not our body, it's mine.>>

Amelia snorted. <<Why should I help you if that's your attitude?>>

<<Because you have a choice,>> Tate said, trying to sound persuasive. <<Me or Charlie. It's as simple as that.>>

<<Yago and I could form a partnership,>> Amelia said coldly. <<Work out an agreement with our old friend Charlie. A three-way split.>>

<<There's one problem with that plan,>> Tate said.

<<Oh?>>

<<Yeah, Yago hates your guts.>> Tate made it sound like a fact. She wasn't sure it was.

<<Yago is shrewd,>> Amelia said confidently. <<He'll make the deal that's best for him.>>

<<Amelia's right,>> Yago said bitterly. <<I'm shrewd, I'll cut a good deal. I'm with Tate.>>

<<You'd turn complete control over to her?>> Amelia shrieked. <<I didn't allow her to eat me so that I could become a prisoner! I want to be human again! I want independence — not this awful half-life. Yago, if we work together, we can achieve that.>>

<<Two words,>> Yago said. <<My neck. Your tongue! And don't forget — no food! You totally betrayed me, Amelia. I wouldn't make another deal with you if you were the last disembodied life-form on this stinking tin can.>>

"Wh — what?" Charlie mumbled in a confused, sleepy tone. Their screaming fight — the only kind they could have — had finally awakened him. "What are you guys doing?" he asked with a soft giggle. A rhetorical question. "Forming coalitions?" He began to laugh harder. "Trying a little diplomacy, Tate?"

Tate didn't bother to answer. She settled in to think and to wait for the next time Charlie fell asleep.

The days with Charlie in charge took on their own rhythm. Early in the cycle, he would spend hours searching Daughter's databases for information about the American Civil War. He was obsessed with the Battle of Antietam. Or, as Yago called it, the Battle of Tedium.

He'd skip dinner because around that time he'd be busy singing the few Motown hits he could remember. Target practice began after dinner and lasted well into the night. He changed Mother's course daily. "To keep them confused," he explained. Nobody but Charlie knew who "they" were.

On the fifth night, Charlie came very close to puncturing the hull with a machine gun blast as he ran through the ship doing a poor imitation of the Rider battle cry.

<<Fine,>> Amelia said as soon as Charlie had passed out. <<We'll do it your way, Tate.>>

<<What's the plan?>> Yago asked.

<<We have to kill Charlie without harming my body,>> Tate said.

<<Neat trick,>> Amelia said. <<We don't have any weapons. Or any way of using a weapon even if we did have one.>>

<<We're going to attack him psychologically,>> Tate said.

<<You mean drive him mad,>> Yago said flatly.

<<Yeah,>> Tate agreed.

<<How?>> Yago asked. Again, his tone was neutral.

<<Ignore him,>> Tate said, feeling terrible about

the cruelty of her suggestion. <<Make him believe he really is all alone out here.>>

<<The silent treatment,>> Amelia said thoughtfully.

<<Yes.>>

<<That could take a long time,>> Yago said.

<<Yes.>>

<<We may go crazy before he does,>> Yago said harshly.

<<I don't think so.>> Tate wanted to reassure Yago. <<We could talk to one another at night, when we were certain he was asleep.>>

<<No,>> Amelia said. <<Charlie could trick us too easily. No, if we're going to do this, we have to commit completely. No talking until Charlie is dead.>>

Tate felt a chill imagining all of that silence. It would be like being dead herself.

<<When do we start?>> Yago asked.

<<Now,>> Amelia suggested, <<before we lose our nerve.>>

Tate showed her agreement by saying nothing.

Three cycles later

*   *   *

"Weakness," Charlie said, feeling devilish, planning to be as insulting as possible. "The weakness is unmistakable. It's the first thing you notice. My old body was much more powerful. I was always having to hold myself back, control some impulse coursing through my muscles. A desire to smash someone's head or pound a tennis ball through my neighbor's window or — well, Yago, you know what I mean."

Charlie chuckled uneasily. He paused — hoping Yago would join in.

Silence.

Charlie took a deep breath and went on. "This body feels so — calm," he said, his voice slowing down as he carefully considered what he was saying. "Weak and calm. Weird, right? You wouldn't expect those two to go together."

Charlie trailed off. This conversation — this monologue — wasn't going at all the way he'd planned. He was starting to creep himself out. That had been happening a lot lately.

He sat quietly.

The immense ship stretched out on all sides of him. His ears strained for some sound, any sound —

He heard nothing.

"Yago, please," he whispered. "Talk to me."

Nothing.

"Tate, please, I can't stand this." Charlie could feel the silence swallow up his words.

Nothing.

Charlie took a deep, shaky breath. "Amelia? Amelia, are you there? Amelia, please —"

Yago was right.

It took longer than Tate had imagined. Much longer.

It was the most dreadful part of Tate's life, and that was saying a lot. She missed her dreams dreadfully.

There were days when Tate's thinking mind disappeared. When she believed she was truly just some sad part of the mutated human named Charlie.

There were days when she'd almost convinced herself it was time to break the silence that had dragged on and on. She wasn't sure what stopped her from giving in.

Desperation.

Competitiveness.

Fear.

Shame.

How could she face Charlie when she knew her silence was slowly driving him mad? Better to stay hidden until he was dead. Better to never speak of what she had done to him.

Better not to think of how very long it took.

Charlie knew the others were still there.

That was what was so infuriating.

They were like a persistent itch that you can never quite find and so you scratch your arm and nothing and twist around to try and reach that spot on the middle of your back and you finally manage to pop your shoulder out of the socket and reach it and nothing and so you try your belly and — the itch is still maddeningly real and yet unreachable.

And so your fingers keep scratching, moving over your skin even after it's raw and bleeding.

You can't give up.

You itch.

And itch.

And itch.

And —

Finally, it was over.

Finally, Tate was able to reach out with her mind and take control of her body again.

She had a mouth. She could talk. "Ollie, ollie, all come free," she whispered.

Silence.

Tate's heart nearly stopped from fear. And then —

<<Hi,>> Yago said.

<<What now?>> Amelia asked.

And then they were all laughing.

CHAPTER FIFTEEN

THIS WAS A DREAM.

20,842 cycles later

Tate stood calf-deep in black goo — a sticky, oily mud that covered this entire nameless planet. Okay, it wasn't entirely nameless. Tate called it Gooville.

She hated the tarlike stuff. Somehow it always worked its way into her boots and drenched her socks. Back on the ship, she'd have to scrub for hours to get it off, and the rotten excuse for soap Daughter produced always gave her a rash.

Still, Tate crouched down in the goo, keen for any movement. She ignored the ache in her thighs, her knees, her back, her neck. The pains had accumulated slowly over many years. They were almost like a background hum she didn't notice anymore.

<<There!>> Yago said.

"I see it," Tate said happily. She watched as a bug the size of her hand leisurely poked its horned face into the air like a dolphin surfacing to breathe. Its front claws looked lobsterlike as it hauled its shiny body out of the goo.

Tate pulled a camera out of her exploring suit and snapped a few photos. She couldn't see the bug's face from where she was standing. With effort, her knees popping, she pulled her boots loose from the clinging goo and scurried around in front of it. She wanted all the angles.

"Was the shell this shiny last time?" she asked.

<<I think so,>> Yago said. <<We can double-check against the files back onboard, of course, but I'm almost certain.>>

"I'm not," Tate said. "I remember writing down 'dull black,' and this definitely isn't what I'd call dull."

<<You remember?>> Yago asked doubtfully.

"It wasn't that long ago," Tate said.

<<Twelve years ago,>> Yago said.

"That long?" Tate tried to ignore how the years had begun rushing by. The speed frightened her.

<<Let's go back and check right now,>> Yago challenged with mild enthusiasm.

<<Why bother?>> It was Amelia.

For a moment, Tate and Yago were stunned into silence.

As usual, Yago was the first to recover. <<Amelia,>> he said warmly. <<How nice to hear your voice.>>

Tate was also pleased.

Amelia had been silent for at least ten cycles, maybe more. Tate had gotten used to her pouting over the years, of course, but the long silences still worried her. After Charlie — well, Tate didn't understand how Amelia could bear to be silent for so long. Of course, it was still her only means of protest, of punishment.

<<This whole enterprise is ridiculous,>> Amelia said with disgust. <<Dull, shiny — what does that prove?>>

"Evolution often makes surprising moves," Tate said patiently. She chose her words carefully, not wanting to say the wrong thing and force Amelia back into silence. "A change in the shell's sheen could suggest a great number of adaptations —"

<<So *what?*>> Amelia exploded. <<If we wait long enough, do you think these bugs are going to evolve into humans? Or any kind of advanced life-forms?>>

"No," Tate said wearily.

The old arguments. Amelia hadn't wasted any time bringing them up. Tate felt a great sadness well up. Amelia was their pessimist — no, worse: their existentialist. She never let Tate lose herself in her experiments for long without pointing out how useless they all were.

<<Sixty years,>> Amelia said coldly. <<In sixty years we've traveled maybe a billion light-years and visited how many planets and moons —>>

"I don't know," Tate said quietly. "As many as we could find."

<<Some bacteria and a mud-dwelling bug,>> Amelia said angrily. <<That's what we've found in sixty years of dedicated searching. When are you going to give up and admit the universe is hostile to life —>>

<<The Shipwrights,>> Yago said, playing the role of Tate's defender as always. <<Humans weren't the only advanced life-forms, we know the Shipwrights —>>

<< — were castaways,>> Amelia interrupted. <<Living on a ship that eventually expelled them — just like the universe eventually destroyed Earth. Let's imagine these bugs manage to evolve into something bright enough to tie their own shoelaces.

My bet is that a volcanic eruption, plague, or cosmic storm would come along not long after and wipe them out.>>

Tate didn't argue. She couldn't.

Amelia had a point.

Tate had spent sixty years searching the universe — more than three times longer than she'd lived on Earth. She'd learned the universe was a big and empty place. The messy human civilization on Earth had been a more precious thing than anyone had ever imagined. Even Attbi had turned out to be empty, dead.

"We'll just have to keep looking," Tate said sadly as she began to pack up her camera and notes. The bug had long since vanished into the goo. It might be hours before another appeared and Tate's knees weren't up to the wait.

<<Looking where?>> Amelia asked, a challenging note in her voice.

<<We have charts,>> Yago began. <<You know that. Several sections of the quadrant —>>

<<Why not go to a planet we know can support life?>> Amelia burst out.

Tate sighed as she slowly made her way up the ramp and into the ship. She suddenly found herself wishing Amelia had remained silent. What was the point of going over the same ground again and again?

She preferred to look forward to a long bath. The goo was already crusting in her boots. Field-work took a lot out of her these days. Not surprising, considering she was nearing her eightieth birthday. She sat on her bed and peeled off her filthy socks.

Over the years, she'd transformed the bridge into a more human-friendly space. She'd gotten rid of some of the old Shipwright furniture and re-placed it with what she needed — a bed, a bath-room. The viewscreens were still there and so was a chair that allowed her to control Daughter. She rarely ventured into the other parts of the ship now. It had been years, maybe even a dozen years, since she'd visited the basement.

Tate was lost in her own thoughts, hardly paying attention to Yago and Amelia's banter. Then she re-alized they'd grown quiet. They were waiting for her to answer a question she hadn't heard.

"What?" she asked irritably.

<<Why can't we go back to Earth?>> It was Yago asking, not Amelia. Yago — who had always been her defender. Tate was stung. Yago had be-trayed her. After all these years.

"We can't go because I don't want to go," Tate said mulishly. She was aggravated to be having this conversation yet again. Why couldn't they just accept the way things were?

The discussion made her feel like a petty tyrant. Yago and Amelia couldn't do anything but nag her. They couldn't go anywhere she wouldn't take them. Well, too bad. Earth wasn't on the itinerary.

<<Tate,>> Yago said quietly, patiently, earnestly, <<I want to see Earth again one more time before I die.>>

Tate froze in the middle of untying her boots. *This* wasn't the old argument. Yago was taking them in a new direction. Tate stared at the floor — and then flung her boot across the room. It looped through the air and landed harmlessly.

"Why?" she yelled angrily. "Why go back there? What's it going to prove? You — you're hoping some green Eden is waiting for us there and it's not, it's not! All that's waiting for us is devastation! It's only been sixty years. Nothing will have changed!"

<<I've changed,>> Yago said softly. <<When we visited Earth last, I saw only devastation. But now, after seeing all of those empty planets — to see even the relics of a civilization . . .>>

<<Sometimes I think I imagined the whole

thing,>> Amelia admitted. <<Movie theaters and Krispy Kremes and fried clams — it all seems so improbable —>>

"Enough," Tate said with disgust. "This isn't an argument, it's nostalgia."

<<What else would you expect from an old man?>> Yago asked.

<<Please, Tate,>> Amelia said simply. <<We may not have much time left. I'm homesick.>>

"Well, snap out of it," Tate said. "I said we're not going and that's final. Now, if you don't mind, I want to take a bath and rest."

<<I won't mention it again,>> Yago promised. <<If only — can you tell me *why* you don't want to go? Are you afraid to face the — the remains of the other Remnants?>>

Tate didn't answer. "Daughter, a bath!" she roared instead.

Yago didn't press the issue. Perhaps he guessed she'd never answer his question.

She couldn't tell him. Telling him would mean giving up the one secret Tate had successfully kept from Yago and Amelia for all these years.

Her dreams.

Her dreams had kept her alive.

They'd come to her regularly for sixty years. She'd walked with the ragged bands of people thousands of times. Sometimes the dreams were indecipherable. Sometimes they were sad. But often they were hopeful. And, occasionally, she dreamed of the green Earth, of Jobs and his children, of a society born again on Earth. A dream like that could sustain her for weeks. She fed off the joy. If she went back to Earth, she'd be forced to admit that her dreams were just that — dreams.

That was never happening.

The sorrow of it would kill her.

The dream came again that very night.

One part of Tate's mind was aware of her body, sleeping aboard Mother, the goo still caked under her fingernails. Another part of her brain was on Earth, the good green Earth.

Billy was there, looking as young and fragile and strange as he had on that day long ago when they'd gathered to board the *Mayflower*. He was holding her hand gently and leading her through a lush forest. They were barefoot. Twigs and ferns and tiny saplings broke under their feet. Leafy trees towered overhead. Tate heard crickets and birds and the chirping of chipmunks. The air was warm and moist on her skin, the thousand tones of green soothing to her eyes.

She'd never had this exact dream before.

It was lovely.

Billy led her to a clearing and Tate saw Mother. She had no sense of surprise. Her dreams were always haunted by the same elements, recombined in endless ways. Billy, the ragged band, Mother. The same pieces shuffled over and over.

This time, in this dream, Mother was nothing more than a ruined hulk, half-submerged in humus and vegetation. A huge hole was torn in her hull, exposing the bridge.

Mother crashed on Earth. That was part of the puzzle.

Billy squeezed Tate's hand and pulled her forward. They climbed up a small crumbling embankment of soil the wind had piled up under the ship and stepped into the bridge.

Tate saw that Billy's face was heavy with sadness. She tried to step back. She didn't want to have a sad dream. She wanted one of the sweet, idyllic ones. But Billy shook his head vigorously and pushed her on.

Tate stepped reluctantly onto the bridge. She saw the forest was claiming Mother, burying her, hiding her. Vines grew over the consoles. Mushrooms sprouted on the soft cushioning of the seats. A bird of some sort had built a messy nest of sticks above the door.

Seeing this, Tate's chest ached with longing. The simple organisms humans took for granted, or even despised — the spores, the fungi, the bacteria — Tate had spent most of her life searching for them in the dead universe. They seemed precious to her now.

Tate turned to Billy. "How can you be sad here?" she asked. "This is glorious! This is life!"

With a heavy slowness, he nodded toward one of the Shipwright's chairs, toward a lump or clump of — *something* she hadn't noticed because the bird's nest and the mushrooms had claimed her attention.

Tate moved closer. More puzzle pieces. She wanted to understand. She, too, knew her time was short.

Some rotted colorless fabric with a darkish stain underneath. It moved faintly, undulating in an unseen breeze. Tate leaned forward and pushed the material aside.

A body. A human body. Two arms, two legs, a head.

Dead.

Tate stepped back, her hands hovering in front of her mouth.

Someone had died sitting in one of the Ship-wright's chairs on Mother's bridge. Nobody had come to claim the body. Nobody had slipped it back into the Earth and hid it out of sight.

What was that?

Tate caught sight of something gray, coarse, fuzzy. It looked like hair. It looked like *her* hair, her nearly eighty-year-old hair.

No. No, it couldn't be.

One of the band. That had to be it. One of the band had gotten onto the ship and died. Of course, none of the people she had dreamed about had kinky hair like hers. None of them were African or African American.

But — so what!

This was a dream. Mother wasn't on Earth. She hadn't crashed. Tate couldn't possibly be looking at her own final resting place. She turned to flee. She didn't want to contemplate her own corpse.

Billy was right behind her. Tate stopped running

when she realized he was moving toward the corpse. She recoiled as he leaned over it and gently pressed his lips to its skull.

"Thank you, Tate," he whispered. "You were always the most generous of the Remnants."

CHAPTER SIXTEEN

"HE'S GONE."

Tate felt terrible when she woke up. The images from her dream — the corpse, Billy's kiss, his words — were still storming through her mind. And her body felt lousy. Her limbs were achy, her throat scratchy. She felt like she was coming down with something.

"Oh," Tate moaned before she even sat up.

<<Serves you right,>> Amelia scolded her. <<You spent too much time chasing bugs yesterday. You're not as young as you used to be.>>

"I'm aware of that," Tate said dryly. She groaned as she sat up and swung her stiff legs out of bed.

"Why are you in such a foul mood?" Since the voices in her head weren't able to sleep, she often woke to an argument in progress.

<<Yago,>> Amelia said irritably.

Well, yes. Who else?

"What did he say now?" Tate asked, mustering her patience. Sometimes Yago and Amelia behaved like two ill-suited roommates.

<<Nothing!>> Amelia raged. <<That's the problem.>>

"Come on, Yago," Tate urged halfheartedly. "What's your side of the story?"

Yago was silent.

Tate felt a flash of irritation. Bad dreams, the flu, *and* the silent treatment from Yago? Beautiful. She couldn't remember the last time she'd felt so awful.

The ship was completely free of disease-causing germs. So, on second thought, this couldn't be the flu. It was probably sore muscles, a touch of arthritis. God, she felt terrible. She hadn't been this sick since — when? Right after Charlie died? Decades ago.

<<Aren't you a bit old to sulk?>> Amelia asked.

An easy opening. Tate doubted Yago could resist the temptation of pointing out that Amelia was the queen of sulking — and that she was several years older than he was.

Yago was silent.

Tate experienced a cold flash of fear that made her stumble on the way to her chair. Yago was dead. Suddenly she knew it was true. He — he must have felt something. He must have known the end was near. That was why he'd made that comment the day before. He'd known . . .

Tate was having a hard time breathing. She was alone now with Amelia. Only Amelia. And who knew how long Amelia would live? One day, possibly one day quite soon, Tate would find herself entirely alone in the empty universe.

"He's gone," Tate whispered.

<<Yes,>> Amelia said. <<I think I know that.>>

Tate felt as if she had killed him all over again. He'd asked her to take him to Earth, and she'd refused. Perhaps he simply couldn't stand the disappointment.

All that long and sad day, Tate sat on her bed and told Amelia what she could remember about her dreams.

Amelia listened. She asked questions. And she began to help Tate solve the puzzle.

It took them seven cycles to decide what to do and another 544 cycles to figure out how to do it.

Some of the things they needed to know were there in Daughter's database.

Other things they needed to know were beyond human understanding when those databases were created. So Tate and Amelia worked on finding the answers themselves. Tate's patience helped. So did Amelia's intellect and her deep knowledge of physics.

And the dreams.

Many of the answers came from the dreams.

The puzzle pieces fell slowly into place.

Tate plotted a complicated course, their last, on the day of her eighty-first birthday.

She and Amelia were waiting, seventeen cycles later, when Earth loomed up in the viewscreens. They could see firelight. A few civilizations clung to the coastlines in Europe, Africa, and South America.

Not new civilizations.

Old ones.

Because Tate and Amelia hadn't just traveled through space, they'd traveled back in time. The year wasn't important. The only important thing was that the Rock wouldn't hit Earth for centuries to come.

North America was still largely dark, home to only a few thousand Native Americans. Somewhere out in space the asteroid was winging toward the planet, destined to wipe out all of the beautiful green and blue.

But now, Tate was convinced, there was a vanishingly small chance that all that devastation could be — not avoided, but undone. She was planting one of the tools to undo it before it ever happened.

"Daughter, identify the continent of Asia," Tate said.

"Identified."

"Accelerate," Tate said.

Mother began to shiver from the speed. Tate and Amelia saw a golden fire around the viewscreens as particles from Mother caught fire as the ship entered the atmosphere.

A few traders felt the impact of the crashing ship.

Tate died instantly. Amelia lingered for a moment longer and then her consciousness also blinked out.

K.A. APPLEGATE

REMNANTS™

Begin Again

"EARTH WILL FALL OUT OF THE SKY!"

So. Billy was alive. Just when 2Face thought she was rid of him forever, he shows up, all spooky glowing superhero guy, speaking in tongues or whatever, sending messages to the masses.

Superhero! What Billy looked like was a dead bug stuck in amber.

And Jobs looked like he was about to burst with happiness. Sanchez was acting all serious and devout, especially after his little fainting drama. Even Mo'Steel seemed in awe of the freak that was Billy.

2Face was furious. No, she was enraged. Her body felt engorged with anger.

She was definitely about to explode. If she didn't get out of that stinking ship —

"I'll be outside," she murmured to no one, then turned and strode from the ship.

Once outside, she breathed deeply, trying but failing to calm herself.

Something cheesy was going on.

First off, why should she trust this Sanchez guy? For all anyone knew he was a total quack. Spiritual seer, her . . . He was probably making up the "message" he heard Billy speak for his own sneaky motives. What those motives could be, 2Face wasn't sure, but that didn't matter.

Anyway, if Sanchez wasn't lying about having received a message from Billy, if Billy really had told him something, then Billy was the one with something devious up his sleeve. Stranding them all — accidentally or not — on this stinking chunk of planet wasn't enough. No! Not for Billy the Weird. He probably had some additional torture in mind.

2Face looked back at the ruined ship and imagined the freak inside. God, how she loathed that guy! *I will stop you dead, Billy*, she vowed silently. *I will stop you cold.*

Newton followed 2Face out into the dusky light and tried to calm his breathing. If he'd stayed inside a minute longer he was sure he'd have gone crazy.

Everyone who had waited outside stopped what they were doing and looked at him. Balder took a step toward Newton, but Newton was in no mood to talk about what he'd seen. Scowling at his crew, he stalked off alone.

The skeleton had been terrible. Newton had heard of Her, the Source, all his life. Seeing Her so up close and personal, though, that was tough.

But far worse was that spooky kid hanging in midair. That kid and all that stuff about a new world! It was all probably a trick, like that little kid who could blend into the dust.

All a trick meant to fool the Marauders.

Newton was used to the dim, consistent light. The ashy ground. The kill-or-be-killed code.

Newton knew his world. He did not want to be thrown into a new one unprepared. So right then and there, looking back at the motley band preparing their nomadic camp — Aga and the other women unpacking food, Croce bullying the younger children, Cocker on guard against danger — Newton decided that he would stop the new world from coming.

The resolution gave him heart. Already Newton felt better, more confident, less — scared.

Life was already nasty and unfair! Look at what

had happened with the kid Mo'Steel! By rights Newton should be leader of the Marauders, not that
stranger.

But he could deal with that — he would deal
with it. For now. Another opportunity would come
and Newton would seize it. He would get rid of the
kid and life would be fine again.

But only if everything else stayed the same.

Newton began to walk back toward the
makeshift camp. Along the way, he plotted. He was
sure he still had Claw, Snipe, and Balder on his side.
That was a place to start. He'd talk to them right
away, tell them his intent to stop that disgusting —
thing — hanging inside the old ship from regreening
the planet.

Whatever that really meant.

Violet found herself seated next to Sanchez for the
meal. Since leaving the ship he'd spoken to no one
and kept to himself. Violet was surprised he'd joined
the group now.

"The visions," he said suddenly, handing her a
small plate of food.

"What?" Violet blurted. "I'm sorry. You took me
by surprise."

Sanchez lowered his head but Violet saw that he was scanning the circle of hungry people. She guessed he didn't want anyone to overhear their conversation.

"Yes?" she whispered. "What about the visions?"

Sanchez hesitated a moment before going on. Finally, he said, "I was afraid of what I saw."

"Tell me," she urged.

Sanchez did.

When he was finished, Violet touched his leg. "But there's nothing to be afraid of!" she whispered reassuringly. "You saw my world. What used to be my world, back before the Rock. Maybe . . . Sanchez, I think you saw what this world will be like someday. Someday soon, if we can believe Billy."

If we can understand Billy, she thought, experiencing a moment of anxiety. So much was up to Sanchez . . . Could he handle it? Would he handle it?

"There is more about the vision," Sanchez said now, poking idly at the food on his plate. "There was a yellow ball. And then it became darker, yet still — intense. Many colors I have seen only in the pillars of flame spread out from it. I didn't know what was happening. The fiery ball began to drop and I thought it would crush Earth but — it just slipped away. Almost immediately, I saw in its place a bright orb. . . . It started to ascend, so slowly. . . . In it, I saw shadows, but they did not dim the brilliance. . . ."

Violet felt her heart swell. She could hardly keep from shouting with joy.

"Sanchez, you saw the setting sun and the rising moon! Wasn't it beautiful?"

Sanchez put his plate on the ground. Suddenly he looked terribly weary.

"I don't know," he said softly. "I don't know."

"Hey, Sanchez!"

Newton was sitting at the far side of the circle, directly opposite Sanchez. Jobs averted his eyes as Newton dug into his mouth with a grimy finger.

"J'ou tell us a story, something we laugh at," the big man went on.

Before Sanchez could answer, Mo'Steel got to his feet and said, "I've got another idea. We heard something pretty wild not long ago. The Source spoke to Sanchez and he told us all about it. I don't know about you," he went on, looking at each face in turn, "but I've got some questions about this new world."

A murmur of agreement rippled through the

group. Newton, though, was silent and scowling. Jobs guessed he wanted to forget about what had gone down in the old ship.

Like that was possible. Mo'Steel was smart to get people talking. To get them comfortable with a seriously mind-blowing notion.

Aga spoke. "I don't know what to think. But I want to know."

"Me, too," Olga added helpfully. "But where to begin?"

"With what we know of Earth before the Rock," Violet suggested. "We start with the big picture and work down to details."

Mo'Steel looked at Jobs. "How about a lesson," he said. "Explain — simply — some basic science. Basic astronomy. Basic, Duck."

Jobs rolled his eyes at his best friend. "Yeah, I get it," he said. He gestured for everyone to move back several feet. Then, with the back of his spade, Jobs smoothed and patted down a section of ash.

"I'm going to draw some pictures," he said, looking around at the group of wary Marauders. His gaze flickered to Echo, Lyric, and Mattock, then to a few of the *Mayflower* people. "Some of you might be familiar with what I'm going to show."

Stupid thing to say, he realized too late. Half of the Marauders shot dirty looks at the Alphas and Remnants. He'd just reminded the Marauders that he knew more than they did.

"I need a lesson," Noyze said with a laugh. "I was terrible in science class. Maybe I can finally learn something."

Jobs gave Noyze a quick, thankful smile. With the tip of his spade he drew the solar system as it had been known before the Rock. He pointed out Earth and the other planets. He showed them Earth's moon and sun. Next to the crude diagram he drew another one to show what it meant for a planet to spin on its axis. Then he illustrated a planet's path of rotation.

"So, if Billy is talking about a newly green planet, Earth might begin to spin again," he said, becoming lost in the thrill of his work. "To rotate around the sun, too. Which means night and day, and phases of the moon, and high and low tides, and —"

"Spin!" Curia cried. "Earth will fall out of the sky!" Jobs looked up, startled, to see the young Marauder woman climbing to her feet. "We will fall off Earth!"

A murmur of horror swept through the group.

"No, no!" Jobs said. "You don't understand.

That's not the way it works. There's gravity and . . . Look, I know it sounds scary but — trust me. I —"

"Why we trust j'ou?" Nesia shouted. "J'ou talk crazy."

Jobs looked pleadingly at Mo'Steel. His friend walked into the center of the rough circle and with his foot wiped away Jobs's drawings.